For F... rich,
... ...on
... f
...nent,
...chief...or
murder

PAY FOR A VISIT…
DIE FOR FREE

"You need to make money on guests?" Chief Walker replied with surprise.

"Are you suggesting that's illegal?" Mr. Prinney put in quickly. "Mr and Miss Brewster are not idle sloths on the fabric of society," he said. "Why should they not make their home available to paying guests?"

That took the policeman down a notch. "It isn't illegal," Walker replied. "It's just odd. And it's the odd facts that often unravel a crime."

"Has there, in fact, been a crime?" Mr. Prinney asked.

"Oh yes," Chief Walker said. "Your guest was strangled—strangled quite effectively."

Other Grace and Favor Mysteries by
Jill Churchill
from Avon Books

ANYTHING GOES

JILL CHURCHILL

IN THE STILL OF THE NIGHT

A GRACE AND FAVOR MYSTERY

AVON BOOKS
An Imprint of HarperCollins*Publishers*

AVON BOOKS
An Imprint of HarperCollins*Publishers*
10 East 53rd Street
New York, New York 10022-5299

Copyright © 2000 by The Janice Young Brooks Trust
Excerpt from *Estate of Mind* copyright © 1999 by Tamar Myers
Excerpt from *Creeps Suzette* copyright © 2000 by Mary Daheim
Excerpt from *Death on the River Walk* copyright © 1999 by Carolyn Hart
Excerpt from *Liberty Falling* copyright © 1999 by Nevada Barr
Excerpt from *A Simple Shaker Murder* copyright © 2000 by Deborah Woodworth
Excerpt from *In the Still of the Night* copyright © 2000 by The Janice Young Brooks Trust
Excerpt from *Murder Shoots the Bull* copyright © 1999 by Anne George
Library of Congress Catalog Card Number: 99-96769
ISBN: 0-380-80245-7
www.avonbooks.com
Jill Churchill can be reached at **COZYBOOKS@AOL.com** and **COZYBOOKS@EARTHLINK.net**

First Avon Books paperback printing: May 2000

Avon Trademark Reg. U.S. Pat. Off. and in Other Countries, Marca Registrada, Hecho en U.S.A.
HarperCollins ® is a trademark of HarperCollins Publishers Inc.

Printed in the U.S.A.

WCD   10 9 8 7 6 5 4 3 2 1

Chapter 1

Lily Brewster was standing by the gatehouse entrance to Grace and Favor Cottage. "Cottage" was a serious misnomer because the home was an enormous, if somewhat run-down, mansion that overlooked the Hudson River. A brisk wind from the west brought the smell of the cold river water swirling around the mansion, blowing snow from the roof and making the trees in the heavily wooded area to the sides of the mansion creak and groan.

Lily was waiting, as she'd been doing nearly every day for several weeks now, for the postman. She was huddled in a sable coat that was even more run-down than the house. Her father had bought it for her shortly before the Crash of '29— when the Brewster family was still the financial and social cream of the crop.

She also wore a pair of old overshoes she'd found in the rabbit warren of third floor rooms when she and Mrs. Prinney started cleaning them out a month earlier, and a hand-knitted cap in

1

rather violently conflicting colors that Mrs. Prinney had knitted her for Christmas. But she was still shivering.

She was about to give up when she heard the approaching racket of the old Model T the postman drove in the winter. In summer those who expected to get mail had to go to Voorburg-on-Hudson to pick it up at the post office, which was a cubbyhole in the back of the greengrocer's store. But in the worst winter months, a driver delivered it to the mansions on the hills above the town. It was the town council's way of thanking the few affluent residents who stayed in winter and contributed to the faltering economy.

Not that Lily and her brother Robert were still among the affluent, quite the opposite, but they did live in a mansion, and few people knew their true circumstances.

"Morning, Miz Brewster. Got a bunch of things for you. Jack Summer sent up a newspaper, too," the postman said, handing her a wad of papers, envelopes and the newspaper. "And I brought Mrs. Prinney that roast she ordered from the butcher. He said you could pay whenever you were in town next."

Lily thanked him, tucked the butcher-paper wrapped roast under her arm and hurried inside. She delivered the roast to Mrs. Prinney, shed her fur coat and sat down in the entry hall to look at the rest.

There were a couple letters for Mr. and Mrs. Prinney (by this time Lily recognized their daughters' handwriting). The *Voorburg-on-Hudson Times* headline grabbed her attention next. FRANKLIN ROOSEVELT TO RUN FOR PRESIDENT. Though raised as a dedicated Republican, Lily was glad to hear the confirmation of the rumor. She had no idea what Governor Roosevelt, a neighbor a few miles away at Hyde Park, thought the solution to the financial crisis in the country was, but it was clear that President Hoover was only making things worse. She set aside the newspaper to read the rest of it later, and came to a letter addressed to her and Robert.

She feared it was yet another rejection. That's all she'd received so far, but she was bound to get an acceptance soon. From somebody.

She opened the envelope carefully and read the enclosed card.

"Robert!" she shouted. "Robert, where are you?"

A voice drifted down from the second floor. "Up here. What's wrong?"

Her brother Robert came bounding down the stairs a moment later, a bit disheveled and alarmed—a combination that did nothing to harm his startlingly good looks. He had rather longer hair than was quite stylish, but the dark gloss of it against his fair skin and sky-blue eyes was his own style. Lily, his younger sister, had the same coloring, but not quite the perfection of features that he possessed. A trick of genetics that she considered highly unfair.

"Nothing's wrong for a change," she said. "Something's very right. Come into the library and read the letter I just got. Julian West has accepted our invitation!"

"Julian West? Really?"

"Read this!" she said, shoving him into a chair and handing him the note. "Isn't he absolutely gracious? To be a famous author and write to us in such a friendly way. It's amazing. And look, he signs it 'Julian' just as if we were old friends."

"Don't swoon so, Lily. This was probably written by a secretary."

"I don't care. He's coming here in April. Now we can invite the others. What a coup!"

Lily and Robert Brewster had grown up in the lap of luxury. Their father had been a multimillionaire by the time he was thirty, partly by inheritance, largely by hard work and intellect. But when the stock market crashed and he jumped out of his broker's window five flights above Wall Street, they discovered that he had gotten greedy. He'd borrowed against all the family properties—the apartment in New York, the summer house in Massachusetts, the sprawling home on the coast of South Carolina, the cottage in Kent, England, where they frequently spent Christmases with British cousins. And he had put all the money into the stock market on margin.

After his death, when everything was sold for far less than its value to meet his debts, Lily and Robert were left with their mother's pier glass, eight hundred dollars, and two trunks and a suitcase each of their personal belongings.

And very few skills that meant anything anymore. Knowing which fork to use for shrimp and the rules of polo were no longer valuable assets.

Then almost two miserable years later good luck struck them. Or rather, glanced off them. A very wealthy great-uncle they barely remembered died and left them Grace and Favor Cottage. But Great-uncle Horatio, being both canny and suspicious, had put a huge restriction on them. They had to live in the mansion for ten years without being away more than two months total a year before it actually became theirs to keep. And to prevent them from going back to their useless, rich society life, he left his vast fortune to them under the same conditions.

Uncle Horatio's attorney, Mr. Elgin Prinney, was charged with the duty of disbursing necessary funds for the upkeep of the mansion and grounds, and keeping a close eye on Lily and Robert to see that they observed the rules.

After the first month they'd lived at Grace and Favor, settled in and incidentally solved the mystery of their Uncle Horatio's murder, they cast about for a way to make money.

Getting jobs locally was impossible. Not only did they lack the expertise for working at the butcher shop or millinery shop or boat repair company, but what few jobs there were had already been grabbed by natives of the area who were hanging on to them for dear life. They'd considered traveling by train to New York City for jobs but the train fare would have eaten up any profit they might have eked out. Besides, Mr. Prinney had warned them that there were other relatives who were down and out who might find out about the restrictions in the will and claim that the hours Lily and Robert were working away from home would count against the time they were allowed to be away.

On the first cool day of September, Robert sat Lily down in the morning room and said, "I'm about to perish of boredom and so are you. The Duesenberg is now at the point of absolute perfection and you've read every novel in the library— some of them twice to my sure knowledge. We have nine years and eleven months to go. What are we to do now?"

"We've talked about taking in boarders," Lily said listlessly. "Lord knows we've got enough room here to put up a lot of people if some of them don't mind living in the servants' quarters on the third floor."

"And do you want to be the kitchen skivvy and me be the guy who tries to fix the plumbing and wiring?"

Lily shuddered. "You and electricity in the same breath scare me to death. It wouldn't be much of a life. Oh, Robert, I'm still such a snob," Lily admitted. "The thought of filling the house with railway workers and apprentice butchers makes me cringe."

"Then let me suggest Plan B," he said with a grin. "We have a wide range of acquaintances who still—God knows how—have plenty of money. Why not have guests instead of boarders? People we used to know. People who aren't worried about where the next meal is coming from. People we might still have a few things in common with. Even the most obnoxious guest eventually leaves, but a annoying boarder is hard to get rid of, I'd think."

Lily considered. "I doubt that our old friends would consider us, poor as church mice, to have anything in common with them anymore."

"They needn't know that. I doubt that any of them would go to the trouble of looking up Uncle Horatio's will. They'd just see us as having inherited a big monster of a house in a terrific setting and assume there's a fortune that came with it and that we've gotten greedy about increasing it."

"But they have their own monster houses. Why

would they pay money to come to ours? They'd have to pay, you know. How would we explain that part?"

"I've got that figured out, too. Have you ever been to the Catskills?"

"Not that I remember."

"I have and I had a swell time. Over there they take guests into hotels and even their houses and they provide entertainment. The wealthy Jewish families in the city often spend whole summers there."

"Entertainment? What sort of entertainment?"

"Oh, musical shows and comedy acts and swimming and boating and lectures."

Lily frowned. "But the people we know have all that at their disposal anyway."

"But they don't have—wait for it, Lily—*celebrities*. Imagine if they could come here and spend a friendly week with Dorothy Parker or Sinclair Lewis or Amelia Earhart?"

Lily laughed. "I don't think a week with Dorothy Parker would be a whole lot of fun." Then she added, more seriously, "And we don't actually know any of those people except by reputation. How would we get them to come?"

"Lily, you don't read the newspapers like I do. People like that gad about all over the place. Showing off, mostly. We just write and invite them to visit for free in a great mansion."

"And they'd do that?"

"They might. We won't know until we give it a try."

Lily thought for a long moment. "Back when we were rich, I'd have loved to have shared a private

house for a couple days with someone like Sinclair
Lewis. I love his work."

"I've convinced you?"

"Not entirely. But it's an appealing idea, I have
to admit. The person you have to convince is Mr.
Prinney. There would be a considerable investment
involved."

Lily was always the one who thought about
money. Robert regarded not having it as an incon-
venience. Lily considered losing track of a single
penny a criminal act.

"What for? We've got the house, all we need is
a few celebrities. Classy celebrities, not the Marx
Brothers. Celebrities that snobs like you would
like."

"Yes, but the house would have to be more elegant. What we've got is a lot of rooms and furniture under dust sheets. We'd need lots of fresh bed
linens, lots of cleaning help. Dozens of nice towels
and a full-time girl to wash them. And Mrs. Prinney would never get out of the kitchen having to
feed that many people. Think of the cost of food.
And the cost of getting her helpers for the cooking."

"Mrs. Prinney is never out of the kitchen now,"
Robert argued. "She practically lives there and Mr.
Prinney has already agreed that the kitchen is a
disgrace and needs to be expanded out the back of
the house. And the guests would be paying for the
food and the service. We couldn't start right off,
but we could be planning now for spring. Mrs.
Prinney would love having kitchen girls to boss
around and you and I could swan about as host
and hostess."

"Oh, Robert, it would be fun, wouldn't it. I just don't know—"

"Let's think about it for a while before we spring it on Mr. Prinney," he suggested. "He thinks like you do. You need to line up all the objections he's likely to have and we'll plan how to counter them."

Mr. Prinney bubbled forth objections like a veritable fountain when they brought up the matter a month later. And Lily was prepared for all of them. "What if you can't get a celebrity to come here?" he asked.

"Then we'd have a very up-to-date boarding-house," Lily said.

"It would cost an extraordinary amount to really fix the house up well enough to impress the class of people you're thinking of inviting," Mr. Prinney said.

"But that's a good investment, isn't it, improving the house? Isn't that why you're adding on to the kitchen?"

Mr. Prinney huffed. He knew perfectly well that he was allowing that expense for his wife's sake, not the Brewsters. And he knew they knew it.

"Where would you get the extra help you'd need?"

Lily almost laughed at this. "If we offered jobs, we'd have people lined up for them clear down the road. So many people are desperate for paying work. Including Robert and me."

Mr. Prinney massaged his silly little moustache.

"Mr. Prinney, you must correct me if I'm wrong," Robert said, "but I think Uncle Horatio's real purpose in giving this house to us but no money with it was to make us prove we could be worthwhile business people instead of society bums. He'd have been pleased to see us making our own money *from* the society bums."

Mr. Prinney nodded. "You may be right. I'll think about it."

"Think about it while you look over these numbers I've prepared," Lily said, handing him a stack of sheets with carefully thought out costs and possible profits.

In the end, he agreed to the plan, albeit with great reluctance and on only two-thirds of the expenses Lily had proposed.

Then the real work started. All the many large and medium-sized bedrooms on the second floor were inventoried and cleaned thoroughly and the dust sheets put back on to keep them pristine. Their maid-of-all-work, Mimi Smith, who was a fanatic housekeeper, was given that title and a slight raise and put in charge of purchasing cleaning materials and hiring as little extra help as possible. Lily and Robert both pitched in and learned how to really clean things for the first time in their lives. Fortunately, Great-uncle Horatio, or perhaps his Aunt Flora before him, had a mania for bathrooms. The second floor had at least one tiny one for every two rooms.

"This is not a talent I would have wished for," Robert groused. He had the heavy work of moving the furniture. "I'd rather be daintily dusting furniture. Dabbing here and there with a clean rag. With style and grace."

"Don't let Mimi hear that. She's an expert duster and considers it the very heart and soul of housework. I don't think you grasp what a wonder she can make of an old table with a soft cloth and a little beeswax."

When the second floor was done, they moved to the third. This was attics and servants' quarters and required the biggest investment as there were no bathrooms.

"We're not asking nice people to use chamber pots!" Lily was driven to very nearly screaming at Mr. Prinney when he got the bid for the plumbing and went haywire.

"Nothing wrong with chamber pots," he said.

"Plenty wrong with chamber pots," Robert said with a terribly charming smile. "Would you like for me to enumerate the problems?"

They settled on two bathrooms on the third floor, one large nice one for women, one more modest-sized one for men at opposite ends of the central hall, even though Mr. Prinney wanted to save money by putting them side by side.

"Ladies don't like to be seen and, if you'll forgive me for being rather vulgar, 'heard' in the bathroom," Lily said, her snobbishness in full flower. She was developing a fine sense of what would embarrass their keeper into submission.

"Very well. It's only money," Mr. Prinney said with what he foolishly considered devastating sarcasm.

Lily started sending out invitations to various celebrities for a party the second weekend in April. Amelia Earhart wrote a very pleasant note saying she would be preparing to be the first woman to fly solo across the Atlantic in May and couldn't take the time. Lily would treasure the note in spite of her personal disappointment.

Sinclair Lewis responded that he was working

on a new book that was due at the publisher in June.

They had struck out entirely on their first round of invitations.

And another thing cropped up unexpectedly.

"You know what you're planning is the weekend of The Fate," Mrs. Prinney said.

"The Fate?" Lily asked. Surely rock solid Mrs. Prinney, the best cook in four counties, wasn't into some spiritualism.

"You know. The town party."

"Oh, a fête."

"That's what I said. It's always held on the grounds here."

"What's it like?"

"Everybody brings picnic lunches and there are games and contests and races and the like. The schoolchildren sing and anybody who can play an instrument comes and there's a bonfire and dancing in the evening."

"What do we have to do?" Lily asked warily. Were they expected to be hosts? To provide food and drink and issue invitations?

"Not a thing. Just let people in to use the facilities. Miss Flora started the tradition when she was a young woman, I hear, and even Mr. Horatio, your great-uncle, kept it up."

"Then it will be good free entertainment for the guests," Lily said. She almost added the word 'bucolic' but decided that might be offensive.

But as the winter commenced and the news of the Depression became worse, Lily wondered if anyone would have the money to spend come spring. The economy of the country was deteriorating at an alarming rate. In small towns respectable citizens broke into grocery stores in angry, starving mobs. Nothing so violent had happened in Voorburg-on-Hudson yet, but it could. Last summer there had been one heartbreaking family living at the town dump. Now there were dozens of people, huddled in ragged clothing, constantly crawling over the refuse for anything that could be eaten or sold.

And when Lily and Robert went to town, there was a mood of anger and revolution that hadn't been obvious the previous year. Everybody had thought the Crash of '29 was the low point, and the good life was sure to resume. But it kept getting worse. There was even a cell of Communists who met in ill-disguised secrecy in the back room of the town library once a week. The Brewster family had a second cousin who had been in Russia during the Revolution and amazingly survived. The horror stories he told about what anarchy really meant were terrifying.

But for all that, Lily held out hope. She and Robert no longer lived in a fifth floor walk-up cold-water flat in a dreadful part of the city. Maybe good fortune would come to others in time.

But not until President Hoover was out of office. Lily knew as well as anyone that he hadn't personally caused the Crash, but he hadn't any idea of how to solve the problem either.

Chapter 2

Lily had included Julian West in her list of potential "celebrities" with serious reservations. He was highly unlikely to come or even bother to respond, but she wanted so much to meet him and considered a stamp a small price to pay for even the most remote possibility. But he was said to have a new book coming out in the spring and might wish to finally end his reclusive style of life.

She was giddy with astonishment and pleasure when he accepted the invitation. Even Robert, who wasn't as devout a reader as his sister, had read and enjoyed most of West's early books, though he didn't like the more recent ones, was downright excited.

"Who shall we invite as the paying guests?" he asked.

"I can think of dozens of people who would regard meeting him as a real coup. Addie Jonson, for one."

"Your old gym mistress?" Robert asked, rolling his eyes.

"No, you're thinking of Miss Adams, the horrible gym mistress. Addie was the literature teacher at

14

my school. She's the one who got me reading Julian West's books in the first place. It would please her enormously to meet him. I don't know that she can afford it though."

"She still has her teaching job, hasn't she?"

"Yes, I got a letter from her only last week saying she'd turned down the offer to be headmistress because it would cut into her teaching with trivial nonsense about kitchen help and obnoxious parents."

"Lily, we're doing this to make money," Robert reminded her.

Lily nodded. "I know. And she knows our situation. She's probably better off than we are, come to think of it. She owns several little houses near the school that she rents out."

"Who else comes to mind?" Robert asked, relieved that the monetary aspect was settled and that Lily, the financial whiz, wasn't going gaga and sappy.

"Cecil Hoornart," Lily said.

"Who on earth is that?"

"He's reviewer, critic, biographer and professor at Columbia who was a guest speaker at our school when we were reading West. He knows West's work well and has probably never met him."

"A critic? Won't West storm back to his hideyhole when he learns a critic is among the guests?"

"I don't think so. Professor Hoornart loves his books. When we could still afford to take the paper, he always reviewed them very favorably. And I'd like to invite Raymond Cameron and his sister Rachel as well."

"Raymond Cameron!" Robert groaned. "Holy

Toledo! I thought you'd gotten over that wet rag a hundred years ago."

"He wasn't a wet rag. He was very smart and I've been over him, as you so rudely put it, for a long time. I only thought of him because he was always a reader of current literature. And his sister Rachel is very beautiful and ornamental. You'd like having her here. And I hear they're still madly rich."

Lily thought back to high school when she was friends with Raymond. And in spite of her denial, he *was* a wet rag. Homely, pimpled, bespectacled and shy. But they had been thrown together when he offered her a ride home to the Brewsters' Gramercy Park apartment and when the car broke down, they had over an hour to kill before being rescued.

Raymond had filled the time by talking about books—talking with what Lily thought then and now was wisdom and wit. Being an avid reader herself, Lily argued some of his points and agreed with others. For several months before graduation, they managed to meet to exchange books and commentary on them.

There was no romance to it, just two good young minds having a meeting. At least, that was Lily's view. And when, on graduation night, Raymond proposed that they give up college and run away and get married immediately, she was appalled. And being too young and inexperienced to cover her reaction or think of a good answer, she simply said, "No, Raymond. I don't want to marry anybody for a good long time. You're a good friend, but . . ."

He'd turned and walked away. And she'd never

seen him since. But she felt a lingering desire to get in an apology for her youth and stupidity and thought the lure of one of his favorite authors might bring him to Grace and Favor.

"Lily? Come back," Robert said as Lily stared out the window of the big library. "You've got Addie Jonson, this critic bloke, and maybe the Camerons. That's only four people. Don't we need at least five or six to astound and amaze Mr. Prinney with the plan?"

"I'll think of two more to invite and another two to put on hold in case the Camerons won't come. Trust me, Robert."

"Don't you wonder at all why West agreed to come here?" Robert asked. "Recluses seldom accept invitations to meet with a bunch of strangers."

"I do wonder. I suppose we'll find out in good time."

Addie Jonson and Cecil Hoornart immediately and enthusiastically accepted the invitation to visit and to pay a fee for the pleasure. To Lily's surprise, Raymond and Rachel Cameron also sent acceptance and a check as well. Lily dithered a bit. What would she say to Raymond? Apologize for her rejection or just pretend it had never happened and that they were merely old acquaintances?

She would have dithered a great deal more about it if she'd had time. But time was at a premium. There was too much planning and work to be done on Grace and Favor. The maid, Mimi Smith, had "assigned" Robert to the master suite when they first arrived the previous August to take up residence. It had been Great-uncle Horatio's rooms and before that Horatio's Aunt Flora's rooms and before that . . . who knew?

Robert hated the bedroom, which was huge and dark, with big pieces of furniture that lurked like ponderous animals at night. He tried to claim that the gigantic sofa had red eyes in the dark that watched him sleep. Nobody believed him, but he stuck to the story.

There was an adjoining dressing room, long and narrow and equipped with a bed, wardrobe and sink for a personal servant. There was also a huge bathroom with a tub one could easily house a family of five in.

Robert suggested they try to lighten up the room and let him take another so that the honored guest, and perhaps his valet or secretary, could have the room. Surely such a famous person would have a servant of some kind he'd bring along.

The walls were paneled in a dreary greenish oak. Or maybe it only looked green because of the heavy vegetation outside the small windows. Had they the skills, they might have removed the paneling to sell, but instead they reluctantly painted it a slightly yellowish-white and had a tree cut down that obscured the view of the Hudson River beyond the lawns behind the mansion. It was a huge improvement. The Oriental rugs scattered about the room suddenly came to life in brilliant greens and whites, and the furniture, which had looked like hulking brown bears and buffalos, was revealed as being a lovely tan shade.

"Now I'm sorry to have given up the big room," Robert said, studying the bedroom at the other end of the hall that he'd chosen.

"Too late to go back," Lily said.

She was doing the arithmetic in the journal she'd bought to keep track of expenses. With the four guests, they could afford to feed Julian West and anybody he might choose to bring along. They needed only one more guest to make a profit. Two would be better.

Robert was full of suggestions. Bad ones. Most of his friends were the polo and nightclub circuit set. Mental lightweights, in Lily's view, though she was careful to express it more tactfully.

"Idiots, you mean?" Robert asked cheerfully. "Sometimes an amusing idiot is a lot more fun to be around than brainy folks."

"If this works out, I promise you idiots next time," Lily said.

Chapter 3

The next guest Lily acquired was a surprise.

She got a note from a woman she vaguely remembered from her "previous life," as she and Robert called it. Lorna Pratt, now Mrs. Ethridge, writing an elegant hand on superb stationery, wrote to say that she had heard through her good friend, Addie Jonson, that Miss Brewster was hosting Julian West at her home with a few select invited guests.

"I knew him when I was very young and greatly admire his work," she said. "I know this is terribly pushy of me, but might you have room for one more guest?"

Lily had only a fleeting memory of the woman, who had come to one of her mother's garden parties when Lily was a child and wasn't much interested in adults. The only thing that she remembered was that the woman had been extremely well-dressed and pretty, and had seemed pleasant.

Lily wrote back, saying Mrs. Ethridge would be a welcome addition, but made quite certain that the uninvited guest understood it was a paying proposition.

"This is the one where we make a profit," Lily told Robert, who was playing a game of patience at the library table. "And we still have room for another. Several others, in fact, but I think the first time it would be a good idea to keep it to six guests plus the celebrity. That's enough people for pleasant conversation with each other, but not a mob. We don't want to scare off our first famous person by having a swarming herd of people demanding his attention. Especially since he's such a reclusive person."

"Aren't you even curious about that?" Robert asked. "Why did Julian West, of all people, agree to this?"

"You sound downright suspicious, Robert."

"I suppose I am, a little. I can't quite put my finger on what motive he might have for coming here, but I don't quite like it."

"Robert, this isn't like you." Lily said, moving his ace of spades to the side of the other cards.

Robert slapped her hand away. "I like keeping it there until I need the space. Maybe I'm just bored into inventing trouble where none exists. How about Mad Henry Trover?"

"As a guest? Mad Henry? This is a joke, isn't it?"

"Mad Henry is fun to have around."

"Mad Henry is a drunk," Lily said.

"He doesn't drink at all," Robert said. "He just has a naturally exuberant personality. I like Mad Henry. Always did."

"Does he still have money?" Lily asked.

"Wads. Tons. It falls out of his pockets and rolls across floors. People follow him around picking it up. His father discovered that gold mine, you remember, then considerately dropped dead so Mad Henry could have his toys. The villagers at The Fate will love him."

"You're saying it like Voorburg does," Lily said with laugh. "But Mad Henry? I don't imagine he knows what a novel is."

"Probably not, but I'd enjoy catching up with him," Robert said.

Mad Henry considered himself an inventor and always had one or another peculiar project that he was engaged in. Lily found Henry annoying and remembered vividly the time he'd visited them for the summer in Nantucket and decided to rewire the house with something he claimed was a new metal of his own creation. It took the whole family, staff and several neighbors with buckets of seawater to put the fire out.

"He's given up anything to have to do with combustion, I hear," Robert said, laying out a new hand of patience. "I think there must be a card missing. I can't seem to win."

He sounded so pathetic that Lily gave in. "All right, invite Mad Henry. But you're in charge of him if he gets out of hand."

Robert grinned. "He's really smart, you know. Most of his projects don't work out, but someday he'll invent something good."

"Better than the suspenders?"

"He didn't think he invented suspenders. He just made them easier to pack," Robert said, laughing. "Instead of them getting all tangled up, they were a series of stiffened wood bits that could be folded up neatly like a carpenter's rule. And what's more, you could change the color just by painting them."

She liked it when Robert laughed. He'd always been so good natured and since they'd come here, he was marginally less cheerful. If it took putting up with Mad Henry to make him happy taking in a bunch of intellectual guests that would probably bore him senseless, so be it.

Lily didn't read the newspapers that Robert and Mr. Prinney did, but she read the Voorburg newspaper carefully. Not only was America in trouble, but the rest of the world was going to pot as well. In January German Chancellor Bruening declared that Germany would not resume its payments for war reparations. She found it frightening that Germany was getting haughty again. And later in the month there was an article about the Japanese attacking Shanghai and Manchuria. That wasn't good news either. And in early February a man named Hitler became a Nazi candidate for President of Germany. Some people were encouraged by this, but most who followed international news more closely than she did, said he was a man to be feared.

But in spite of the world situation, the work on Grace and Favor continued to be Lily's main concern. The third floor plumbing was almost finished by the end of February and Lily and the housekeeper Mimi Smith were cleaning out the small rooms on the third floor that had been servants' quarters in the past. One of them was unfinished and was full of old suitcases and trunks. The first trunk they opened turned out to be packed with old-fashioned women's clothing, all carefully wrapped in tissue paper. It looked like the clothes of a young woman. Had it been Uncle Horatio's

Aunt Flora's clothing? She would have been born in about 1850 or so and would have put up her hair and donned a corset as an adult just after the Civil War. Oddly, the clothing looked more modern than that, although Lily knew little of what girls wore that long ago.

Another trunk had "grown-up" clothing that was certainly Flora's. Crinolines, horsehair hoops, high-necked dresses in modest, if not drab, colors. The sort of clothing Queen Victoria would have approved of. A third trunk contained costumes. At some point in the history of the mansion, there had been parties that called for guests dressing up as monks and Spanish pirates and famous queens.

That probably wouldn't be appropriate for the gathering they were planning, but later perhaps.

If there *were* to be parties later. If this one didn't work out and produce a profit, however small, she and Robert would have to take in boarders instead. And there probably wouldn't be costume parties with boarders.

The future suddenly loomed large, long and boring.

"I'm going to the post office to send an invitation to Mad Henry," Robert said the next morning. "Want to come along?"

Lily had to go to town to pick up some groceries that had been inadvertently left out of Mrs. Prinney's order, and she was eager for any excuse to get away for a bit, so she took him up on the offer. Robert drove the Duesenberg, but refused to stay around. "I've got some other things to do as well," he said, trying to impart an air of mystery to himself. "I'll pick you up in half an hour."

"It won't take me that long. I just have to stop by the butcher shop."

"Then waste some time at the hardware store. It's the best heated building in town," Robert said. "I'll scoop you up in the Duesie there."

Robert dropped her off and went on his way. His errand, not as mysterious as he'd made it sound, was only to go to the *Voorburg-on Hudson Times* newspaper office for a gossip with Jack Summer, the young man who was the editor. The newspaper office was the second warmest building in Voorburg and Robert was curious about some new neighbors three houses along the upper road from Grace and Favor Cottage.

Lily headed for the butcher shop and found that there was a sale of really pathetic pork chops that didn't even look edible, but had drawn a crowd. Because she hated the cold, damp, dead animal smell of the shop, rather than wait in line she decided to make another visit and come back when the pork chops were gone.

On one side of the town square, there was a millinery shop. Lily couldn't afford any new hats, but she loved looking at them and trying them on. Those that were displayed in the front window were quite nice, if a bit dusty. But the displays inside the shop were lovely. A young woman came out from a workroom at the back of the shop. She was little and pretty with somewhat fuzzy strawberry blonde hair pulled into an old-fashioned Gibson Girl sort of hairdo.

"Miss Brewster?"

"How did you know me?" Lily asked.

"Somebody pointed you out at church once. I'm Phoebe Twinkle."

"Oh, the sign on the door of the stairway next door has your name on it for tailoring and alterations, doesn't it?"

"Yes, I do the hats down here and the alterations in my room above the shop. Must make ends meet, you know. I have the perfect hat for you. Two or three, in fact."

Phoebe lifted the flap of the counter and came around and dragged Lily over to a dressing table with three mirrors, tilted in such a way that a customer could examine how a hat looked from all angles.

"I'm not really shopping," Lily said, loath to admit that she couldn't afford a new hat. "I'm just waiting for the crowd to clear at the butcher's and I've been anxious to meet you."

"The ptomaine pork chops? Even I wouldn't eat them. Don't worry. You don't have to buy a hat. It's a slow season and I welcome the company. Be right back."

A moment later, Miss Twinkle reemerged from the back room with an armload of hat boxes. The hats were, to Lily's surprise, very beautiful and stylish. "They're gorgeous!" Lily exclaimed. "Where did you learn to do this?"

"I used to work in a very fancy shop in Chicago. But my aunt, the only family I had left, became ill and I came back here to Voorburg to care for her. Bless her memory. Poor as a church mouse, but the dearest old thing in the world. I thought I might as well stay here and set up my own shop. That was in early 1929. I had no idea then what was going to happen later in the year. My aunt died the day of the Crash."

"So did my father," Lily said, then wished she

hadn't. "Is your last name really Twinkle?" she asked to change the subject.

"In a way," Phoebe said, adjusting a floppy-brimmed straw hat with gauzy trim to a more flattering angle on Lily's head. "My great-great grandfather came here from Amsterdam with a name that not even the other Dutch could spell or pronounce. It must have sounded a bit like 'twinkle' so he just let himself be called that. This hat is really you."

Lily was spared answering by the little bell on the front door jangling. A terribly thin, smiling woman poked her head in the shop. "Phoebe, dear, Mrs. Cox's flour sifter is jammed and I thought I'd just slip upstairs and take the one I left behind here. I told Mrs. Cox you wouldn't mind a bit since you don't do any baking to speak of."

And she was gone.

Phoebe shoved her hands into her hair, seriously disarranging it, and made a little growling noise. "My landlady. Mrs. Gelhaus. She'll drive me utterly mad someday."

"Why is she taking things from your room?"

"Because it used to be hers. Hers and her husband's. This was a bakery and when Mr. Gelhaus died, she went to live with her widowed sister-in-law, Mrs. Cox, and rented the shop and the room upstairs to me. Fully furnished. Then. Not anymore.

"She drops in at least once a week to take away one little thing or another she's decided she needs. There used to be three sets of sheets, now there's only one. Three of the four chairs have disappeared as well. I live by myself so she assumes I can't sit in more than one at a time and Mrs. Cox needle-pointed the seat covers and so dearly wanted to have them as extras for bridge parties." She said this in exact imitation of Mrs. Gelhaus's chirpy voice.

Phoebe drew a long breath and said, "I shouldn't complain."

"You certainly should!" Lily said. "Or take something off the rent you pay."

"I can't. She was my aunt's best friend and I really don't want to get into a tiff with her."

The bell jangled again. Mrs. Gelhaus was back. In one hand she had the flour sifter, in the other, she had a little wooden box with drawers. "Phoebe, I'm taking this tiny chest as well. Mrs. Cox has been dying to have something to put her spices in. She's such a good cook, you know. And you only had a couple spools of thread it in. I put them on the mantel for you. Goodbye, dear."

Phoebe looked like she needed to go have a good cry.

Lily rose and said, "I'm sorry, I must go. I'll come back again though. Thank you so much, Miss Twinkle, for showing me these lovely hats. I'm going to be having guests soon and I'll make sure the ladies come here."

"Thank you, Miss Brewster," Phoebe said, her voice shaking.

Lily ran over to the butcher's, where the crowd had dispersed when the shop ran out of the terrible pork chops. She picked up the overlooked items from Mrs. Prinney's shopping list and went outside just as Robert showed up. Lily threw the packages in and said, "Don't start home yet. I need to talk to you."

Ten minutes later, after a brief discussion, Lily

and Robert went across the square to have an equally short chat with Mr. Prinney at his office in town.

"Nice girl, that Miss Twinkle," he agreed. "And just between the three of us, Mrs. Gelhaus not only takes things from her own house, she's been known to lift a few trinkets from other people's houses. Go ahead."

Lily went back into the millinery shop. Phoebe Twinkle's eyes were red and swollen, but she forced a smile. "Miss Twinkle, forgive me for asking a rude question, but I do have a good reason. What do you pay for the room above the shop?"

Phoebe admitted it was three dollars a week.

"That's an outrageous sum. I have an offer for you. I have rooms bigger and nicer than yours at Grace and Favor, and for the same amount of money, I'd give you the room *and* board. You've probably heard what an excellent cook Mrs. Prinney is. Nobody but the maid will ever enter the room and you can even lock her out if you want."

Phoebe just stared at Lily.

"Where do you normally eat?" Lily asked.

"At Mabel's Cafe."

"I've eaten once at Mabel's and believe me, the food is better at our house and would be included in your rent. The only drawback is that it's up the hill. You'd still have to pay for your shop rental and you'd have to walk to and from work occasionally. Mr. Prinney says he would drop you off in town the four days a week he's in his office and bring you back at the end of the day as well."

Phoebe suddenly put her hands to her face and gave a quick sob.

"I'm sorry. I didn't mean to upset you, Miss

Twinkle," Lily said. "Just give it some thought at your leisure."

Phoebe looked up from her hands. "How soon may I move in?"

"As soon as you like."

Lily went back to the car, where Robert was reading a magazine and smoking one of the rare cigarettes he allowed himself to buy. "We have our first *real* boarder, Robert."

"A little old hatmaker," Robert said, taking one more puff of the cigarette and putting it out very carefully so he could smoke the rest of it later.

Lily laughed. "Little, but not old. Quite a knock-out, I'm happy to tell you."

Chapter 4

"Would the Captain rather sit over here?" Bud Carpenter asked.

"It's a damned train, Sergeant. Where I sit will not influence whether I get there sooner or later."

"Now, now, sir, let's don't be grumpy," Bud said, not intimidated in the least. "I just thought the Captain might like to sit facing forward."

"You peevish old maid! I'm fine where I am," Captain West growled. "Leave me alone, can't you?"

Captain West was a big man, once a handsome one, but running just a bit to fat now in middle age and scarred about the face and neck. The scarring wasn't severe, but it had pulled his once-handsome features a bit to one side, giving him an odd, lopsided visage.

His dark, glossy hair was getting a dusty gray at the temples and a network of angry lines had been overlaid on his face. Most people would regard him as haughty but dignified, a man who wouldn't lightly allow himself to be crossed in even the most trivial matter.

But Bud Carpenter, a slim, stiff, younger man,

31

had known him for most of his own life. He'd been
a paper delivery boy in the same town where the
Great Man lived and had adored him. When Julian
West's first book was published, Bud had purchased it out of his meager funds and read every
word of it, finger following down the pages phrase
by phrase, lips moving slowly with the words. It
was the first book he had ever read voluntarily.

He screwed up his courage and knocked at the
door of the big stone house the day he finished
reading it rather than leaving the paper on the
stoop.

The Great Man had come to the door himself.
"What is it, boy?" he snapped impatiently. "Do I
owe you money? My cousin John takes care of that
sort of thing. But he's in the hospital with pneu-
monia. Come back next week."

Before the door could slam, Bud put his foot over
the threshold. "No, sir, you don't owe me nothing.
But I want to work for you."

"Why?"

Bud hadn't expected the question. He stammered
for a moment, then got out the words, " 'Cause I
liked your book. First whole book I ever read. And
I'm a good hard worker. I can garden and cook a
bit and fix near anything. You got a broken window or a electric light that won't work or a cistern
to be emptied, I'm your boy."

With a rare smile, Julian West said, "Well, neither my cousin nor I is very good at any of that.
Let's give it a try."

Bud had been with the West cousins ever since,
boy and man. He kept the household running
smoothly and was unobtrusive. He accepted Julian's cranky nature as the right of a Great Man who

had a lot of important stuff on his mind and books to write that told you lots of things you'd never of known otherwise.

Cousin John had returned shortly, cured of his ailment, but a bit on the morose side. But Bud accepted that, too. Mr. John West helped the Great Man. Typed up his books, took care of paying the bills and venerated Julian as much as, or even more than, Bud himself did.

Years later, when the Great War came and both West men signed up for the army, Bud signed up along with them.

"You can't do that," Julian had said. "You have to stay and take care of the house."

"Nossir," Bud Carpenter said, drawing himself up to his full height. "I'm going with you. We'll close up the house, or maybe hire some woman from the village to come in and look after it, but I'm going with you. You need me. The both of you do and you know it."

The cousins had reluctantly agreed.

He'd been with them the whole time, being the only one of the trio who came out unscathed either physically or mentally by the horrors of shelling, gassing, gangrene, trench foot; the stink of rotting flesh of young men coughing up their lungs; and the sheer, terrifying boredom of waiting for the next horror.

When the war was over, he'd come back with Captain West and taken up where they'd left off, in spite of the cousin having died in a fire in the trenches. Bud went with West to the nursing home in England, convinced that mere doctors and nurses couldn't take care of the Great Man half as well as he could. And when, six months after the armistice, they came home, he got the house, garden and kitchen back in order.

He ripped out the poppies, which were a bad reminder of what they'd been through, and put in delphiniums. He'd rewired the upstairs rooms, hired a gardener's helper and a cook, whom he supervised, and got on with life while West recovered from his injuries and got back to his writing. He'd engaged a typist and a bookkeeper for the Great Man (Bud knew his own limitations, regarding figures and the typewriters with suspicion, and he still couldn't read without moving his lips). He went right on running the house and, to an extent, the Great Man's life, with undiminished and fearless bossiness.

"I really think you ought to sit facing forward, sir. You know you get sick when you ride backwards and read at the same time," he said now as the train started moving.

"Oh, very well. If it's the only way to shut you up," Captain West said, slamming down the manuscript pages he'd been trying to study and causing them to slither to the floor in disarray.

Bud picked them up, shuffled them around until they were in order and handed them back with a cheerful, "Here you are, sir. Now, remember, you're under orders to be nice and gracious to these people."

Miss Addie Jonson stopped in Fishkill to see if she could find a sandwich with her name on it. She parked her Jordan roadster on a side street. It was the kind of car she'd always wanted, but couldn't afford until the owner, the headmistress of her school, had a minor accident and vowed never to drive again. She'd sold it to Addie at a price Addie couldn't resist, and Addie loved her little car and the freedom it gave her. She drove it skillfully, but cautiously enough to seriously annoy many drivers who got trapped behind her on narrow roads.

Addie was excited to get to Voorburg-on-Hudson and see Lily again and meet Julian West. But she'd started too early and didn't want to impose herself on Lily for an extra, unplanned meal. She was one of the few people Lily had confided in about the Brewsters' dire financial circumstances and it broke her heart. The Depression, as people were calling it now, hadn't hurt her.

Addie had been teaching for a long time now at a school that paid better than most. She had been very frugal with her money from the time she took the job and had invested it in some small pieces of property, prim little houses around the school itself, which in turn she rented to the school for visiting parents, professors, guest speakers and short-time travelers. As she had no husband, children or parents to care for, her financial responsibilities were to herself alone.

She bought most of her clothes from secondhand stores because she didn't give a damn about fashion, cropped her curly hair short so she had no hairdressing costs, and served as a dorm mother to earn a little extra and save paying rent to someone else. On school vacations, she stayed in whichever of her properties was vacant.

She was a tall, rangy, long-striding woman with a voice that was usually pitched to the back row of girls. Lily Brewster had been one of her favorite students because she was bright and worked hard at her studies in spite of not having to *be* anything after she completed her education but an ornament to society. Lily had developed a schoolgirl crush on Addie—why did so many of the girls do that, silly geese?—which had later developed into a real friendship with only a touch of heroine worship on Lily's side.

Addie had visited Lily once at the dreadful tenement and had been appalled at the circumstances to which the young woman and her brother were reduced. Addie had assured her that with her brains and capacity for hard work, things would eventually look up for her, though Addie wasn't sure it was the truth. Then a year later, she'd gotten a letter from Lily explaining that she and Robert had inherited, in a manner of speaking, a large house, but no money, and would Addie please be so kind as to loan her books. The small town library had such a tiny selection of good fiction and she couldn't afford to buy any, but would find a way to pay the postage both ways.

Addie suspected that's why she had been invited to the house party. The common love of books and all of them that Addie had happily sent along at her own expense. Now she believed her own prediction. Lily would survive, maybe thrive, and Addie was happy to spend some of her hoarded money to help Lily and get to meet one of her literary idols.

She was striding down the main street when the smell of food made her remember her destination. She barged into a small cafe, spotted a waitress and called across the room in her school-mistress voice, "Could you toss together a meat loaf sandwich? Lots of mustard, if you please."

* * *

Cecil Hoornart sat down on one of the railroad benches and fished around in his rucksack for his hiking shoes. He'd gotten off the train one stop before Voorburg early in order to walk the rest of the way. Cecil loved house parties—it gave him so much scope for eating, but as he aged, he was getting a paunch, so he'd taken up hiking rather than cutting down his food and drink intake.

He wouldn't have come to this house party, and he most definitely wouldn't have even considered paying to attend, except that one of his longtime ambitions had been to meet Julian West. Cecil had spent three years researching for a biography of the man. It was a challenge, but when he started his first draft, he thought it was going to be his best biography. He'd written to Julian West, even gone to his house once, but had been ignored. The time he steeled himself to knock on the door to West's house, he hadn't even gotten to say his name before the unsuitably gruff young thug of a butler said, "Mr. West is not expecting a guest. He's too busy to see you, whatever you want."

Mortifying.

But maybe not West's fault. He might not know how rude his staff was. And the butler probably didn't get around to posting letters. Cecil had written West a great many letters and never gotten a response. He'd have to tell West about it. The author would be glad to know. And even if he wasn't, he wouldn't dare offend such an important literary critic who held the power to influence his sales. Authors were always very nice to critics. The more prestigious the venue of the reviews, the nicer they were.

Cecil took his notebook and pencil from his

lightly loaded rucksack and made a note to remind himself to mention the butler. Cecil had sent his luggage ahead to the Voorburg-on-Hudson station. He wouldn't be seen carrying a suitcase even for a short distance these days. So many suitcase-laden men of middle age were out of work and living in shelters like the Muni or sleeping on the streets where decent people tripped over them. He did not wish to be mistaken for one of them.

He hoped the luggage had arrived in good order. He had his only full copy of the draft of the biography he was preparing on Julian West in the suitcase. He was highly nervous that it might be lost and had considered leaving it at home in his safe. But he finally felt so strongly that he should be making notes in the margin of everything West might say, that he'd brought the manuscript along. He had, of course, made carbon copies of the earlier draft, but had been lax about it in the final manuscript.

When he finally puffed into Voorburg, sweating and gasping, the large case with his clothes and the manuscript were not at the station. It was a cool day, he'd been sweating rather vulgarly and thoroughly, and suddenly he felt very cold indeed.

"See here, my good man," he said to the stationmaster, who was sitting behind his counter with his feet on it and reading a magazine about cars. "My luggage has gone missing."

The stationmaster, Mr. Buchanan, who was a law unto himself, gazed up slowly and said, "And who might you be?"

"Cecil Hoornart—the literary critic. I'm sure you recognize the name."

"Not that I know. Lemme take a look around."

A train was just coming into the station and two men in cheap blue suits strolled out to the platform to watch the disembarking passengers. Cecil, who kept up with current affairs, knew why this was. Over a hundred thousand federal officers and civilian volunteers were watching roads and train stations, trying to spot anyone who had a chubby, golden-curled baby with them. Charles Lindbergh's son had been kidnapped the month before and hadn't yet been found.

A moment later the door next to the counter opened and Cecil's pigskin bag was pushed through, the brass studs on the bottom of it scraping on the floor unpleasantly.

"Excuse me," Cecil said. "How do I go about getting to Grace and Favor Cottage?"

"Oh, you're one of the Brewsters' guests? Why didn't you say? Mr. Brewster was here to pick somebody up from the train, but nobody got off. Just wait in front. He'll be back for some others in an hour. Big yellow Duesenberg. You can't miss it."

"Is there a place I could get a drink while I wait?" Cecil asked in a progressively more aggrieved tone.

"There's Mabel's, but she doesn't serve hootch to outsiders. They might be the feds and there's a lot of them around just now."

"I meant a drink of water," Cecil said, which was an outright lie. He'd had his heart set on a gin and tonic.

The stationmaster gestured at the water fountain on the track-side wall. "Help yourself."

Cecil got his drink of water and his pigskin case, and found a bench facing the main street. He sat down heavily. He was wrinkled and damp and had misjudged his footing along the way and fallen in some mud. He might not make quite the right impression. He found himself wondering if this trip had really been a good idea after all.

Mad Henry Trover, his almost colorless blue eyes sparkling, his dark, straight hair blowing wildly in the wind, was driving a borrowed truck up Route 9, thinking madly (he didn't mind being called Mad Henry) about his next invention, the parts of which were in the truck bed. He was so enthralled with the concept that he was thirty miles north of Poughkeepsie before he realized he'd passed Voorburg-on-Hudson.

Raymond and Rachel Cameron were in their brand new Stutz Continental coupe, only a few miles behind Mad Henry. They didn't miss the turnoff, however. "I still don't understand why you wanted to do this," Rachel said, not looking up from her fingernails, which she was alternately filing and admiring.

"Because I used to really like Julian West's books."

"You don't anymore?" Rachel asked.

"They've gotten too dark and grim," Raymond said. "But the early ones were superb."

"I wouldn't have thought you'd want to get tangled up again with Lily Brewster, though."

"Why not?" Raymond asked, flipping the butt end of a cigarette out the window.

"Well, she threw you over."

Raymond turned to look at his sister for a moment. "She threw *me* over? Nonsense. It was the other way around."

He said no more about it as there was a road-block ahead and traffic was at a full stop for searches for the missing baby.

Chapter 5

While these individuals were approaching (or in Mad Henry's case, going away from) Voorburg, Lily was in a frenzy of last-minute preparations. She had checked every room over three or four times just that morning. Suddenly she slapped her head and said, "Flowers! There aren't flowers in the rooms."

She tore down the stairs and into the kitchen. "Mrs. Prinney, I forgot to get flowers."

Mrs. Emmaline Prinney, a large woman who obviously loved eating as much as cooking, was tasting her special secret recipe salad dressing and musing about what a mere breath of nutmeg might do for it.

"Flowers?" she muttered, coming out of her cooking trance. "The woods behind here are full of flowers right now. Mainly daffodils and a few tulips just coming in bloom. You might as well pick them before The Fate. The children will pick them otherwise."

"But what will I put them in? Do we have vases?"

Mrs. Prinney took one more critical taste of the

salad dressing, then opened the pantry door. "We do."

Lily saw that the entire top right-hand shelf was crammed with vases. Certainly, they hadn't accumulated during Uncle Horatio's tenure. His old Aunt Flora must have been the floral enthusiast.

"Keep an eye out for ferns, too," Mrs. Prinney said. "A nice bit of greenery goes well with flowers."

"You're ready, aren't you," Lily asked.

Mrs. Prinney looked at Lily, somewhat alarmed. "Of course I am, dear, and so are you. Don't get yourself into such an awful tizzy."

"I know. I know. It's just that it's so important for everything to go well. Your husband will never forgive us the expense of fixing up the house if we don't at least make a little money and get a good reputation for entertaining from this."

"Pooh. Elgin's looking forward to having guests." This was more wishful thinking than pure truth. "Go pick your flowers, dear. And take Robert along. He's in the library and Mimi wants to carpet sweep in there. Agatha has shed all over the rugs."

Robert wasn't only *in* the library, he'd taken it over. He had newspapers all over the large table. "That Jack Summer is a wonder, Lily," he said. "The master of the noneditorial editorial. Look at this issue. See the front page article? President Hoover is still going on about how it's up to private charities and community funds to cure the financial crisis. He claims the Red Cross should take over the burden. And just below it is a quote from the head of the Red Cross saying they don't have the resources and the local chapters will have to deal with it themselves. No wonder this country is in a mess."

"Hoover actually believes the Red Cross should fund everyone in the country who's starving?"

"Apparently so. Now here's another good piece. Jack's quoting a speech President Hoover made last week to a group that had convened to formulate suggestions for ending the financial crisis in this country. Hoover said that they were too late, that the financial crisis was over and everything was rosy. People were going back to work in droves. And instead of making any comment directly, Summer snuggled an article right next to it saying that a recent governmental survey had shown that more than one out of four formerly gainfully employed people is now out of work. Brilliant placement."

"We aren't two of the four at the moment," Lily said. "I need you to come pick flowers in the woods with me."

"We're going a'Maying?"

"We're putting them in the guests' rooms and the public rooms. Please pick up these newspapers. Mimi needs to carpet sweep."

"She does not. You could operate on somebody on this floor. You and Mimi have gone buggy on cleaning." Spotting a clump of fur decorating the rose-patterned rug, he yelled for Agatha, Lily's dog, who had been in hiding under the library table during the height of the cleaning.

"Hmm," Robert said and lifted some of Agatha's fur. "If this is the start of the Spring Shed, Mimi's got her work cut out for her. There's an awfully lot of fuzzy stuff under Agatha's top coat. I never noticed that before. Look at this. You can pull chunks of it loose."

As they headed out the kitchen door with Agatha, Mrs. Prinney handed Lily a large, flat wicker basket.

"What's that contraption for?" Robert asked.

Agatha shot out the door and gamboled around his legs. Robert plucked another clump of fuzzy fur off his trouser leg.

Lily rolled her eyes. "It's a trug. For putting the flowers in, Robert."

He shrugged. "I thought it was a clown hat."

"Oh, Robert," she said, irritated. "And Agatha, if you jump on me one more time . . ."

Robert took Lily's arm and stopped her headlong dash into the woods.

"Lily. Look at how you're behaving. We're having guests. Guests don't like overwrought, hysterical hostesses. They're coming to enjoy themselves, and you've turned, my dear sister, into the least enjoyable person in the world."

Lily glared at him, then relaxed. "You're right. I absolutely hate it when you're right."

"As seldom as it happens, I can see how it disconcerts you," Robert said with a toothy grin. Even making faces didn't destroy his good looks.

Lily heaved a great sigh. "Okay. I'm pleasant now."

He poked his forefingers at the corners of her mouth. "Then look like it, for Pete's sake. Everything's copacetic."

"If you say so. And I *have* noticed Jack sticks those articles next to anything to do with Hoover. It's a real skill at making a point without beating it to death. He was a good choice."

Jack Summer had been the downtrodden reporter on the local paper when Robert and Lily first arrived in Voorburg the summer before. When the incompetent editor went elsewhere, the brother and sister learned that they were the owners of the newspaper. Or would be when they'd served their ten-year sentence at Grace and Favor. They and Mr. Prinney, the estate's attorney, who had the final word, had debated cutting their losses and letting the paper fail or turning the editor's job over to Jack Summer. Mr. Prinney later told them that he'd feared that Jack, being young, brash and untried, might take the failing newspaper under altogether.

Going along with the pretense that Robert and Lily were the actual owners and he was acting on their behalf, he had, however, hired Jack and was surprisingly pleased at the results. In spite of the increasingly desperate financial status of virtually everyone in town, Jack had increased the circulation significantly.

"You *have* invited Jack to some of the festivities, haven't you?" Robert asked, snapping off a daffodil flower and tossing it in the trug.

"Robert, don't just pick off the heads. Pick the whole stem."

"Oh?" Robert looked at the lonely, beheaded flower. "Right."

"I've not only invited Jack to the big Dutch dinner Mrs. Prinney is making," Lily went on, "I've written another note to Mr. West asking permission to let Jack interview him for the paper at his convenience. And I've written to all the guests about the fête as well."

Robert pretended to swoon. "You really are the goat's whiskers, Lily."

She tossed a bunch of new, still tender, half-curled ferns into the trug. "Is that good or bad?" she asked.

"I'm not sure," Robert said, surprisingly serious. "I'm still uneasy about why Julian West, a notable hermit, is coming here."

"I don't care why," Lily said. "I'm just glad he is." But Robert's uncharacteristic worry was starting to infect her, too.

Julian West, the man who had accepted the Brewsters' invitation, was a very famous writer, extremely popular with men readers and even with a smaller group of women who enjoyed military history. He wrote war novels. His earliest, before the Great War, had been acclaimed as "brutal but truthful" and "brimming with the romance and blood of American history."

He'd covered several battles of the Revolution with style, wit and impeccable research. One was from General Washington's point of view, and it was the first time many otherwise well-read people realized that the badly dentured hero had a Great Love in his life who wasn't his wife.

Another of the Revolutionary War books featured Aaron Burr, the hero turned traitor that the public had loved and then hated. And the critics had swooned over his ability to get inside the historical figure's head and make him a little bit sympathetic. That book, titled simply *Hero*, had been a best-seller for nearly two years.

Then he'd taken on the War of 1812 from the joint viewpoints of President James Madison and his wife, Dolley. This had been Lily's favorite of his works. His perceptions of Dolley as she packed up the presidential home and fled with national treasures as the British were literally breathing down her neck were magnificent.

Quite a remarkable feat for a man, Lily thought.

Then the Great War had started and Julian West, the expert in wars, joined the American Expeditionary Forces under Pershing. There was a long hiatus in his books. He was said to have been wounded while attempting to rescue some other soldiers and mildly gassed as well. The wounds, it was rumored, were burns to his face.

He returned home and became a notable recluse. But he had a real war under his literary belt by then, with real experience to write about. His next book was very dark, very brutal, and was the account of a fictionalized officer, believed to be based on his own experiences, though he refused to be interviewed and never admitted which scenes were based on his own life and which were from comrades'.

With the next book he returned to the Civil War, focusing on Robert E. Lee, who had been asked to serve as Commander of the Union Army and, with torn emotions, had turned it down to head the Confederates. But this book, like the Great War book, was darker and more violent than his earliest works. Two more books had followed and his output of work severely slowed. One was set in Roman times and the other was about the French Revolution. He remained remote from the public in his lifelong home in upper New York state.

Lily had thought the chance of his coming out of hiding to get together with strangers was highly unlikely, and now, like Robert, she was wondering why her invitation had enticed him to do so.

*   *   *

Everything was as ready as it could be by three o'clock Thursday afternoon. Mimi was still tidying upstairs, but Lily didn't want to be in work clothes when the guests arrived. They been asked to turn up around four. Plenty of time to unpack, relax and meet one another over drinks before dinner.

Lily was at loose ends. Robert had given Agatha a good brushing outdoors and she was no longer shedding in clumps, only wisps. Lily and Agatha settled in the library, Lily because it had the best view of the Hudson flowing by beneath and beyond the long sloping yard, and Agatha simply because she stuck close to Lily as a matter of policy. Agatha, a mix of collie and something else, had been abandoned and starving when Lily found her in the woods the previous summer and adopted her.

Without anything to do or anybody to nag, Lily let her mind drift. It drifted to her late father, who wasn't someone she normally let herself think about. When he discovered that his great wealth had all vanished in the Crash through his own greed, he had committed suicide. Lily's first reaction had been horror and sadness, but after the pitiful remains of his estate had been settled, she'd become angry.

At first, Lily thought, *How dare Father choose death over Robert and me?* He'd wrecked the only kind of life they'd ever known, and hadn't the spine to face up to it. He'd been a brilliant man and might have been able to recoup in time. And he'd have been a comfort to them and they to him. It wasn't until the will was probated that Lily and Robert realized they'd actually have to get jobs—a totally foreign concept to them.

For almost two years Robert, a devout New Yorker, had worked as a fill-in waiter in the elegant restaurants he used to patronize and occasionally squired rich old ladies—who always introduced him as their nephew—to Broadway shows. They were generous old ladies, but playing the role of gigolo to elderly women was a humiliation to him. Though nobody but Lily guessed that. Robert was an almost unrelentingly cheerful individual who disguised a very good brain behind a slangy playboy facade.

Lily had taken work at a bank downtown in New York City where she spent dreadful long days mindlessly sorting checks and filing them. She had never made friends with her coworkers, downtrodden women with whom she had nothing in common. In almost two years of utter boredom and hard work, the brother and sister were only a few dollars ahead. They shared a wretched tenement apartment on the Lower East Side and a daily horror of winding up in the breadlines.

When Lily saw a notice in the personals column of a New York newspaper urging Miss L. Brewster and Mr. R. Brewster to contact Mr. E. Prinney in Voorburg-on-Hudson, they suspected it was a joke someone was playing on them, but were so frantic at the heat of the city that they took the train to Voorburg and discovered that their great-uncle had left them a mansion and a fortune.

Lily, who was about to be fired from her dreadful bank job anyway, was happy to move to the small town of Voorburg-on-Hudson where the view was spectacular, the surroundings were clean, and she could have a lovely bedroom to herself with her very own elegant little bathroom.

Robert, on the other hand, was a young man who thrived on society—New York City society in particular. A superb polo player, a bon vivant who had never seen a sunrise unless it was at the end of his evening and who was never without a coterie of lovely young women (and the occasional lovely young man) drooling over him, he wasn't prepared for living in a remote mansion perched over the tiny town of Voorburg-on-Hudson.

But in the few months they'd lived at Grace and Favor Cottage, Robert had made a sincere attempt to accept the situation and kept himself very busy tending to the enormous, beautiful, butter-yellow, highly chromed Duesenberg that was also part of their inheritance. This, to him, was the only remaining remnant of the Good Life.

Though they were housed in a mansion, they had no income and no skills at earning a living. Mr. Prinney, the estate's attorney, and his wife moved into the mansion as well, however, and paid a modest room and board fee. Mr. Prinney was their jailor, their boarder, and controller of the funds that would someday be theirs, and he had come to be—in his distinctly proper, prissy way—a friend to them. His wife didn't mind leaving their former home in the town because their four daughters had married and left home and she was lonely for a bustling household. She was a big, hearty woman with a fine appetite whose life revolved around the pleasure she took in feeding people. The more, the better. So she became their cook, and the Brewsters and Prinneys ate superbly well.

Mr. Prinney, who hadn't approved of his client's will, was inclined to be generous in his assessment of what costs were justified in keeping up the house. There was a live-in maid, and normal household purchases—toilet paper, soap, cleaning supplies, all the costs of upkeep and repairs—were paid from the estate funds, which were mainly in land, gold and small businesses. Great-uncle Horatio had seen the crash of the market coming and had gotten out.

Still, while Lily and Robert had a place to live and good food, they had very little money to spend on themselves, and Great-uncle Horatio had made clear in his will that maintenance of the estate didn't include allowances. Lily's and Robert's clothes were out of date, and starting to look very shabby. Lily, who was a great reader, couldn't buy books, and the town library couldn't keep pace with her because the village budget no longer allowed for purchase of new books. Lily couldn't even afford to have her hair done, which she considered a horrible fate. Robert had very few companions and he pined for society, bright lights and bun fights like he used to participate in gleefully at several of his elite clubs.

But over the years, the anger she'd felt about her father had gradually faded to a sort of numb pity. And, surprisingly, a certain amount of gratitude. If things hadn't happened as they did, Uncle Horatio wouldn't have had his sneaky detective keep an eye on the brother and sister. Uncle wouldn't have seen, albeit secondhand, how hard they had worked to keep their heads above water. He wouldn't have had the least faith that they could make themselves useful and productive here in this sprawling mansion.

Of course, this first foray into commerce might prove that they couldn't.

Lily had come to love living in the house, resid-
ing in the small town of Voorburg-on-Hudson, in
spite of the dire poverty most of the citizens were
enduring with anger tempered with bitter humor,
mostly in the form of Hoover jokes. It was better
to be poor in Voorburg than it was in New York
City. A number of people who could ill-afford it
had taken in the children of the even less fortunate.
There were good people in Voorburg.

Lily had discovered since coming to Grace and
Favor that she had a skill for numbers and Mr.
Prinney had been gradually bringing her along in
the many businesses and pieces of property that
were part of the inheritance. While many of the
businesses had gone bankrupt, Mr. Prinney and
Lily had agreed to attempt to keep as many of them
as possible in business. They were, in their very
small way, actively fighting the crush of unem-
ployment, and that made her proud.

The big bakery in Cleveland was doing all right
in spite of some labor leaders making threatening
talk. So were the cattle ranches in Colorado, and
the film studios in California were paying off their
leases quite successfully. The talkies seemed to be
the only thing downtrodden people could find to
take their minds off the Depression.

The steel mill in Pittsburgh was foundering, but
so far Lily and Mr. Prinney refused to lower the
workers' wages and hours even though the demand for girders was falling like a rock because no
one could afford new construction. Money was
pouring into that concern, but not back out.

This wasn't, however, the time to think about
that. She turned her thoughts to Robert, who was
as citified as a person could be. Even he was ad-

justing slowly to rural life. The idea of taking the trouble to bring in interesting guests had probably appealed much more to him than to her. Though she was still a bit fretful about Robert's misgivings about their first famous guest being Julian West. What if West just locked himself in his room and refused to socialize with anyone?

Her musings were interrupted by the doorbell. She glanced at her watch. Only three-thirty. Somebody was very early. A uniformed driver stood at the door, "I'm delivering Mrs. Ethridge, ma'am. This is Grace and Favor Cottage, isn't it?"

Lily confirmed it and he went back to the enormous black car purring quietly in the drive. He opened the back door for his passenger and started unloading a flock of little pieces of luggage.

"You must be Lily," Lorna Pratt Ethridge said, coming to embrace Lily. "The last time I saw you, you were a girl in French braids. And here you are now, a lovely young woman. I'm so grateful you allowed me to force myself on your party. I hope I haven't inconvenienced you by arriving a bit early. My brother needed the car and driver for an appointment later. I knew Julian West when I was a young woman and I'm so anxious to renew our friendship."

Lily had led Mrs. Ethridge into the house as she talked. Mrs. Ethridge looked around and said, "My! This is much bigger and nicer than I would have thought from outside."

Mimi appeared, did a quick curtsey and took the first flood of the luggage upstairs.

While Mrs. Ethridge looked around, Lily studied her. She was a little woman with tiny elegant hands and feet. A bit overweight, but in a lush and attractive way. Her voice, deep and husky for such a small, dainty woman, was appealing as well. It suggested intimacy.

She hadn't succumbed to fashion and had on a rather plain but expensive and well-made dress, and her glossy brown hair was drawn back simply in a thick bun at the back of her head. Her jewelry, of which there was a lot, was small and delicate. She wore a gold necklace with a pendant of grape leaves and tiny, faintly greenish pearls and matching earrings. Several bracelets clinked melodically against one another.

Lily knew that Mrs. Ethridge was probably in her fifties, and looked it, but was very attractive and . . . well, alluring. She was one of those rare middle-aged women who would probably attract even men much her junior. There was nothing vulgar about her, but she seemed to naturally ooze sex appeal in the most refined way.

"Would you like to see the rest of the house?" Lily asked, not quite knowing what else to do with her first, solitary and uninvited guest.

"Perhaps later, dear. It's been a longish trip. I'd like to just sit down somewhere and collect myself first."

"Let's go to the library then. It's my favorite room and has a wonderful view."

They settled themselves in two comfortable chairs flanking a small antique marquetry table. "I remember your mother so fondly," Mrs. Ethridge said. "She was such a lovely woman and it was so tragic that she passed from us so young. How old were you when you lost her?"

"Fifteen. It was very hard," Lily said uncomfortably. She didn't like talking about her mother and her heartbreak to a relative stranger.

There was a tiny rumble somewhere. Mrs. Ethridge waved a dainty hand at her midsection and said, "So sorry, but I didn't get lunch."

"I'm sorry. I'll get you something."

"Oh, I shouldn't ask. It's so rude of me. But . . . if you might have just the tiniest little thing I could nibble on?"

"Of course," Lily said. "I'll have a sandwich made up."

Mrs. Ethridge was distressed. "No, no, dear. Just a tiny plate of cheese and crackers would suit me fine. Perhaps the itsy-bitsiest dab of caviar?"

Mimi had quietly reappeared and was standing next to the library door. "Would you like to see your room now, ma'am?"

"Oh, I would so love that," the older woman said. Then turning to Lily with a blinding smile, said, "You wouldn't mind if your maid brings my little snack to me, would you? I need to freshen up and take a little rest."

"Not at all," Lily said with a gracious nod. "I'll see to the food if you'll take Mrs. Ethridge upstairs, Mimi."

"Caviar," Lily said a moment later to Mrs. Prinney. "The early guest wants a tiny dab of caviar with cheese and crackers." She unwittingly imitated Mrs. Ethridge's modest sweetness and thought, *That wasn't nice of me.*

"Caviar? We don't have caviar until tomorrow night and I don't want to open it up yet. How about a bit of my crab salad?"

Mimi appeared in the kitchen a moment later, looking confused.

"What's wrong, Mimi?"

"Oh, nothing, Miss Lily. I just don't know if that lady is being really nice to me or making fun of me."

Lily thought that was an interesting insight, especially from Mimi, who normally didn't question anybody's manner.

Mrs. Lorna Pratt Ethridge hadn't done a single thing wrong, had been extraordinarily gracious and friendly.

But Lily had decided, almost against her will, that she was going to have to work at liking this guest who had invited herself.

Chapter 6

The next guest to arrive, to Lily's delight, was Addie Jonson. "I'm a bit early," Addie said, "but I was so eager to see you and your mansion. Dear God, it really is a mansion, isn't it."

As they embraced, Lily said, "It's a huge place. I suspect there are rooms I've never yet found. And I hear there's a basement. Only Mr. Prinney is brave enough to go down there and always comes back up with dusty, crusty bottles of wine. Come in and have a lemonade with me. Our Mrs. Prinney seems to be involved in black market for lemons."

"Oh, your lawyer's wife. She does the cooking, right?"

"She lives for cooking. She raised four daughters as hefty as she is and when they married and moved out of the Prinneys' house in town, she missed cooking for them most of all. Now she cooks divinely for us. She can do astonishing things with the cheapest cuts of meat. Come in the library. It's the best room in the place."

They sat for a moment, Lily staring affectionately at her mentor and friend. Addie had on tan trousers; her hair looked like she'd cut it herself without a mirror, all fluffy and frowsy and going a bit gray at the temples.

"Don't worry. I brought dresses along," Addie said. "And even a hairbrush."

"I don't care."

"These are my driving clothes . . . and hair," Addie said with a laugh.

When Lily returned from alerting Mrs. Prinney that another guest had arrived, Addie was studying the bookshelves that lined the walls of the library. "And I've been sending you books when you have so many!"

"Yes, but have you looked at the titles?" Lily said with a laugh. "Really dull stuff. I think someone must have purchased them by the yard as decorations. I'm not really sure they're all really books at all. They might be fake spines. Nobody has yet found the key that unlocks the glass doors."

"You're happy here, aren't you, Lily."

"Very happy. You saw how we lived before in a fifth floor walk-up that was filthy and falling down around us."

"And Robert? Is he happy?"

"He's thrilled to be out of the apartment, but he misses the city and the nightlife and his polo-playing friends. Voorburg doesn't go in for polo. But we do have a movie house where he goes every time the film changes. It's the only business in town that's really thriving."

They drank their lemonade and made conversation for a quarter of an hour, then Addie said, "Come see my little automobile. She's so trim and I love her."

Lily tried to pretend an interest in Addie's roadster, but drew a line at Addie hefting the side panels over the engine and showing her all the lovely parts inside. "Let me help you take your things inside," Lily said.

As they reached the foot of the steps leading to the second floor, Mrs. Ethridge was descending. "Oh, Addie! How nice to see you again, my dear."

She rushed down and enveloped Addie in a hug. Addie stared over the woman's shoulder at Lily with a stunned look.

Mrs. Ethridge gushed over Addie for a few minutes, saying how very well she looked, how long it had been since they'd had a nice long talk and how they must find time to catch up.

Addie said nothing and Lily rescued her. "I must take Addie to see her room, Mrs. Ethridge. There's lemonade in the library, if you'd like some."

"How refreshing so early in the year," Mrs. Ethridge said. "You must tell me how you get lemons. And Addie, dear, we really must make time for a good old gossip."

Lily led the way to the little room she'd picked for Addie. It was rather plain, with simple furniture and a brightly colored quilt on the bed. A small bath and a large closet with a hall between them joined this room with Mrs. Ethridge's. Lily had chosen it especially for Addie as she knew Addie didn't like a lot of girlish clutter.

"It's your room anytime you can get away to visit, Addie. I thought it suited you perfectly."

Addie turned to her, her face pale. "What is that woman doing here!" she exclaimed.

"Mrs. Ethridge? She invited herself. She said you told her about the house party."

"How dare she use my name that way! I've not spoken casually to her for years. She must have heard that I was coming here from someone else."

"Oh, dear . . ."

"I'm sorry, Lily, but I must leave. I can't bear to be in the same state, much less the same house with her."

"Addie, whatever is the matter. She seems so nice in a frou-frou way. Please don't leave."

Addie turned her back, crossed her arms and stood silently for a long moment.

"All right, Lily. I've been looking forward to our visit and I don't want to disappoint you. Most important, I have too much pride to let her run me off."

Lily took Addie's arm and led her to the bed, where they sat down next to each other. "Addie, tell me what this is about."

Addie sighed. "To sum it up, she stole my beau and killed him."

"What!"

"Oh, it's more complicated than that. I don't know why it would interest anyone else, but it's no secret. When I was thirty and already an old maid, I met Anthony Ethridge. He was older than I and had a bad war wound. A piece of shrapnel lodged near his heart and couldn't be operated on for fear of dislodging it in the surgery. Anyway, he had to take things easy and had applied himself to reading everything he could get his hands on."

"An appealing trait to the likes of us," Lily said.

Addie nodded. "Very appealing. I fell madly in love with him. Silly at the great age of thirty, I know. I'd already been teaching for years and liked it, but I wanted to marry. I could have 'done' for him. I could cook, clean, pluck chickens, fix engines, put up shingles. I could have been the perfect wife. And he agreed. He was aging, lonely. I thought he was in love with me. Maybe he was. He bought me a ring, found a nice little house near the school so I could go on teaching, and we set a date to marry."

"Where does the woman downstairs come into this?"

"Between setting the date and getting married. She moved in next door to the little house I was fixing up. Anthony, being in poor health, couldn't help, but he came and sat and watched. Lorna had a lot of free time on her hands and spent it vamping him."

"And he fell for it?"

"Of course. I couldn't really blame him. I was plain; she was beautiful and alluring. I was competent; she was charming. I was younger than he and she was of his generation. It's not as much fun for a man to watch a woman hang a new window as it is to flirt with a charmer. I know that now. I was too stupid to see it then. Anyway, he broke off our engagement and married her. I think he felt as awful about it as I did, but he was enchanted with her. She'd magicked him."

"How did he die? What do you mean about her killing him?"

"It was three years later. They were still living in 'my' wedding house. Anthony was failing. I'd see him in town in a wheelchair. But Lorna was apparently tired of being a nurse by then and took off for a nice long trip to Europe. She'd been widowed before and had tons of money. She didn't even hire anyone to take care of him. If I'd known, I'd have been there for h—"

Addie put her hands to her face and made a horrible sobbing noise. Lily gave her a pat on the shoulder and went to get Addie a glass of water from the bathroom while she pulled herself together.

"Here, take this."

Addie sniffed and raised her head. "It's all right, Lily. I'm all right. I did nothing wrong. Maybe Lorna did nothing wrong. He might have insisted he could get along by himself and refused to have help. It was the sort of thing he'd say. I don't know. It's not fair for me to blame her for his death. Just for her taking him away. And even that—well, if she could take him, so could someone else."

"Stop being so damned reasonable and fair," Lily said.

Addie almost smiled. "But that's what I am, Lily. Reasonable and fair. Stupid of me, I know. I hear automobile tires in your drive. Go see to your guests."

Lily found it hard to put Addie's story out of her mind, but what could she do about what had happened to her mentor and dear friend? The man in question was long dead. She wouldn't let Addie leave if she could help it. The only option was to ask Mrs. Ethridge to pack her things and go. Greed fought with loyalty. And plain old shyness came into it as well. She'd never imagined herself being able to say to a fairly respectable person, "Get out of our house." She wasn't sure she could do it without bursting into tears or fainting.

Meanwhile, Robert, with a big grin on his face, was showing Cecil Hoornart into the house. Mimi was on duty at the door. "You must be Professor

Hoornart," she said. "Let me show you to your room, sir."

Cecil was a bit disconcerted. How did this aging platinum blonde guess who he was? He didn't look, at the moment, the least like the sophisticated, well-groomed, intellectual Cecil Hoornart.

Cecil looked, and feared he smelled, like a hobo. He was taken to a single room on the third floor. Quite a nice little room, he had to admit, with a lovely view of the Hudson River below the grounds behind the house.

"Wouldcha like me to unpack for you?" Mimi asked, as Lily had instructed her.

"No, thank you," he said.

"The bath's at the end of the hall, sir. Has a little sign on it with a man. Miss Brewster says to tell everyone that the bedroom doors only lock from the inside, so if you have valuables, you can lock them in Mr. Prinney's safe."

"I do have valuables, but they are of worth only to me," Cecil said, thinking about his precious manuscript of the biography of Julian West. "I'm waiting for a telephone call from my secretary. Has she rung yet?"

"I don't think so, sir. I'll ask Miss Lily."

It took considerable effort to spruce himself up and he discovered that he'd forgotten his hair oil and so his thinning hair looked fuzzy. He'd have to turn out in his dinner clothes soon, but wanted to meet his host and hostess first, and donned his country gentleman clothes. A tweed jacket—the one with the signature leather patches on the elbows—and tan trousers that were getting just a little too tight for comfort. He'd hoped the walk would have worn off a bit of belly, but it hadn't.

He ran into Lily on the landing of the stairs.

"You must be Professor Hoornart," she said, extending her hand as she came up the steps. "You disappeared so quickly I missed you. I'm Lily Brewster, and my brother and I are so glad you found time to come here. You won't remember me, but you came to my school to lecture once and I've followed your reviews ever since then."

Cecil ran his hand over his hair like a handsome rooster preening his feathers. This was the sort of hostess he liked. One who fawned. Now if the food was up to par, and Julian West would agree to an nice long interview, it would be worth the trip.

He asked her about a phone call. "I'm expecting a letter from a woman who had worked for Julian West's family when he was a child. You know I'm writing a biography of him, don't you? I've asked my secretary to call here if the letter arrives while I'm gone and read it to me."

"If she calls, I'll be sure to fetch you to the phone," Lily assured him.

They exchanged pleasant chitchat as Lily showed him around the main ground floor rooms. "It's a bit of a maze, I'm afraid. Robert and I kept getting lost the first month or so we were here and we suspect there are still rooms we haven't discovered."

"You haven't lived here long?"

"Only since last August," Lily said, gently steering him toward the yellow parlor. "We inherited it from an uncle we hardly knew and it had been rather badly neglected for a number of years. Especially the grounds, which are still being cleared."

The yellow parlor had been selected as the best room for the guests to gather. It had the most comfortable furniture. There were several deep sofas and chairs grouped around the fireplace and scattered in pleasant conversational clusters. Robert was sprawled in one of the sofas reading the newspaper. He leaped up and offered Cecil Hoornart a drink.

"A gin and tonic, please," Cecil said, feeling more at ease now that he was clean and decently dressed and being received with the respect he felt was owed him.

Lily turned as Addie entered the room, looking quite normal. Lily performed the introductions.

"We've met, Professor Hoornart," Addie said, extending her hand to shake his manfully. "You graciously agreed to speak to our girls at school quite a few years ago. That's how Lily, who was a student then, and I knew you."

"So she told me, Miss Jonson."

Cecil had long since given up speaking to secondary schools, reserving his limited time for the best colleges and exclusive dinner meetings at the most elite clubs, but pretended effectively to have remembered Addie. "One of my fonder memories," he said. "And are you still with the school?"

When conversation lagged a bit and Robert was pouring Professor Hoornart a second drink, Lily pulled Addie aside. "I'm going to tell Mrs. Ethridge that she must leave."

"You'll do no such thing. You need her money," Addie said quite firmly in her school-mistress voice, nodding to Robert with a smile as he called across the room, "Sherry?"

"No, Addie," Lily persisted, "not that much, we don't. I don't want her to ruin this visit for you."

"I simply forbid it," Addie said calmly, tipping

her head in thanks as she took the tiny crystal glass from Robert. "I'm over my weeps. I simply need one good cry every five years or so. I can cope perfectly well. I refuse to hide from the woman or have her run off as though I were too delicate to manage. I mean it, Lily."

Without another word, Addie strode back to the fireplace and took a seat next to Cecil on one of the sofas. "I enjoyed your review last week of Edna Ferber's latest book, but I wondered if you weren't a little harsher in your criticism of the setting than you might have been."

Cecil loved defending his often cranky views, and he and Addie fell into an animated and high-minded discussion that made them forget their host and hostess entirely.

Lily was relieved that she didn't have to throw out a guest and breathed a contented sigh as the doorbell rang again. It was all going to be all right. Addie would be sincerely gracious and so would Mrs. Ethridge and very soon the rest of the party would assemble and there would be good food, good talk and an all-around good time for all.

She hoped.

Chapter 7

The next two pairs of guests arrived almost simultaneously, which disconcerted Lily for a number of reasons. Rachel and Raymond Cameron were slightly in the lead and Lily hardly recognized them. Raymond, who had been a skinny, drippy-looking boy in high school, had matured into an extraordinarily handsome man. The rest of his features had caught up with his nose at last, and his formerly short-cropped mouse brown hair had darkened into a sweep of fine, dark, slightly wavy beauty. It was hair that anybody would both admire and envy. The gogglish reading glasses weren't in evidence and for the first time Lily realized Raymond had wonderful brown eyes.

"Raymond! Rachel! How you've changed," Lily exclaimed. "I'd have hardly known either of you on the street. I'm delighted you're here." But she was eyeing the town taxi that had just pulled up. This was the guest of honor and couldn't be ignored.

Fortunately, Robert came to the rescue, and took the Cameron brother and sister off her hands. "We must catch up," Lily said to them before approaching the cab.

Robert did a good job of being a jolly distraction from Lily's preoccupation with Julian West. "Do come in," he said. "The maid will get your bags and show you to your rooms in a few minutes. Come into the parlor and meet the others. And a good drink wouldn't come amiss, would it?"

As he spoke, he kept his gaze on Rachel Cameron, a gorgeous girl to be sure. Amazing how these scrawny little girls sometimes turned into stunning women.

Rachel gazed back with doe-like dark eyes and glanced at his left hand briefly, wondering if he was married. She hadn't heard of a marriage, but then she'd heard very little about the Brewsters lately. Someone had told her they'd gone dirt poor, but if this really was their house, that rumor was obviously wrong. And with money, Robert might make quite a respectable husband. She'd already turned down three proposals, waiting for the right man to come along. By which she meant a man with money, a good heritage, good looks and social connections.

"Just the tiniest glass of wine for me," she drawled, taking Robert's arm. "I have to watch my figure, you know."

"Well worth watching," Robert said with a smile.

Lily, meanwhile, was in front of the house introducing herself to the great Julian West. "We're so very pleased you were able to come, Mr. West."

"Captain West, if you would, ma'am," a gruff voice from inside the taxi said.

"Sergeant Carpenter, stop your maw," West said. "The war's been over for a long time and I'm plain

Mr. West. I'm glad to be here," he added to Lily in a tone that suggested that he'd much rather be home. "This is my man, Bud Carpenter. And you must call him Bud."

"Of course." Lily stumbled over the words. This was going to be more difficult than she'd imagined. If West was already squabbling with his valet, it didn't bode well.

She was somewhat surprised at the look of Julian West. He was a big man in his early fifties, who had the look of just starting to settle into middle age. His brown tweed suit was crumpled, his too-long hair ruffled and untidy. But the overall effect was 'artistic,' she had to admit. Except for the scars on his face.

The flesh of the right side of his face from his temple to his jaw line was slightly shiny, almost hairless and faintly crinkly. Lily assumed this was the result of burns from the war. The skin wasn't very discolored and the tightness of the right side pulled his mouth slightly askew and gave him a vaguely quirky look, as though he was perpetually expressing surprise and a bit of cynicism.

Sergeant Bud Carpenter, who had emerged backward from the taxi dragging luggage and a heavy typewriter case along with him, was a different kettle of fish entirely. He was younger, shorter and had quite a military look with his stiff bearing. The sort of a man who could execute a very snappy salute, she guessed. Carpenter was a man who looked like he might have come from extremely common background and had remade himself by sheer willpower.

"There's a chill in the air, sir. Best get inside," he said, hoisting the luggage with no apparent effort.

"Quit nursemaiding me," Julian West said, as he turned to go into Grace and Favor. Lily couldn't guess if this was a dismissal of his valet or obedience to the younger man's orders.

Mimi was at the door again and tried, unsuccessfully, to wrest the suitcases from Bud Carpenter. "No, miss. No one but me touches the Captain's things."

Mimi cast a quick glance at Lily, who nodded slightly and said, "Mimi, would you show the gentlemen to their suite? And then, Mr. West, as soon as you've rested from your journey, we'd be very grateful if you'd come to the yellow parlor—Mimi will show you where it is—to meet our other guests. They're all very anxious to make your acquaintance."

Why am I talking as though I were in an etiquette class? Lily wondered, almost laughing at herself.

"Hmm," was the only response from the primary guest.

Lily watched as they ascended the stairway behind Mimi and wondered if Julian West would ever come back downstairs. In spite of his moderately polite remarks, he obviously wasn't looking forward to this visit. The typewriter case alarmed her. Did he regard Grace and Favor as a place to hole up and write instead of socializing?

Lily had saddled one of her dearest friends with an enemy who apparently wasn't aware of the clash between the two of them. The guest of honor obviously didn't want to be where he was. Robert was making goo-goo eyes at a beautiful woman he couldn't afford to take even to the moving pictures, and Mad Henry was presumably on his way to Grace and Favor and would likely wreak havoc.

Lily found herself wondering if this had all been a big mistake.

Mad Henry had come across Phoebe Twinkle walking up the road from town, asked directions to Grace and Favor, and offered her a ride upon discovering that she lived at his destination. Phoebe had the impression that he was about sixteen years old. He was small, wiry and youthful-looking. Lily had told her, however, that Henry had been in school with Robert, so he couldn't be as young as he looked.

When they came into the mansion, they were already deeply into a conversation.

"But it's not really terribly practical, is it?" Phoebe was saying as Lily came into the entry hall.

Lily had been darting back and forth from the parlor to the entry at regular intervals. She noticed out of the corner of her eye that Bud Carpenter was standing, as if at attention, at the bottom of the stairs as if he were a member of Grace and Favor's staff rather than Julian West's.

"Practical? The most practical thing in the world," Mad Henry said. "It's exactly what Henry Ford is doing," in his rather high-pitched, boyish voice. "If you make a really good hat, and take it apart carefully, and make a die to cut all the pieces, then you can make endless identical copies on an assembly line. One group of people would lay out the fabric and cut it, the next would put the first two pieces together, the next group would add the brim, the next would put on the net or flowers or whatever you wanted and you'd have dozens and dozens of hats in no time."

"All the same size," Phoebe said with a laugh. "And identical."

"You could make batches in different sizes."

"But they'd all look exactly the same." Phoebe was being very patient.

"Of course. That's the beauty of it."

"Mr. Trover," Phoebe said patiently, "you neglect the human element. Women don't want other women to be wearing the same hat they are."

"Why on earth not? A hat is a hat, just like an automobile is an automobile."

"That's precisely where you're wrong on two points," Phoebe said, hanging up the lightweight duster she'd been wearing. As she brushed some of the dirt from Henry's truck from the hem, she said, "One: a hat is an ornament to a woman, like her jewelry and dress. Her choice should be attractive on her and say something about her taste and style. Two: a car isn't just a car. Your truck is nothing like Robert's Duesenberg."

"Robert has a Duesenberg?" Mad Henry exclaimed. There were three quick, small crashes as the screwdrivers he'd been clutching in one hand dropped to the floor.

Lily stepped into the conversation. "He does, indeed, Henry, and he'd love nothing better than to show it to you."

She fetched Robert, which wasn't easy. He was having a conversation with Rachel, and Lily nearly needed to smack him to get his attention. But realizing that he was going to get to show off the Duesenberg, he abandoned Rachel. As Lily shepherded him along to the front hall she turned to take a quick look back. Cecil and Addie were having an animated discussion by the fireplace,

Raymond was studying a painting on the far wall, and Mrs. Ethridge was showing Rachel something in a magazine. All appeared to be going well enough.

Bud was still in the hall. "May I help you?" she asked.

"No, miss. I'm here to help you if you need me. Captain West said I was to be useful."

"Oh . . . how nice," Lily said, supposing this was really West's way of getting Bud out of his hair. "Would you mind gathering up the empty glasses in the yellow parlor then?"

Bud nodded and went to the task.

Mad Henry had gone out to unload a number of small wooden crates from his truck and Robert was helping him. Phoebe Twinkle was watching them from the door.

"What a peculiar man," she said with a smile as Lily came to stand beside her. "What may I do to help?"

"Nothing that I can think of, except to chat with the others. I'll introduce you to everyone. We do appear to have a few problems you should be aware of. Remember the woman who said my friend Addie had told her about this? Mrs. Ethridge? Well, Addie *didn't* tell her and is very unhappy that she's here. I'd appreciate it if you'd help me keep them from being involuntarily thrown together."

"Will do," Phoebe said, making an elaborate gesture as if pulling two wrestlers apart. "What else?"

"Charm Mr. West. He's obviously not happy to be here."

"Then why did he come?" Phoebe asked.

Lily said, "I have no idea. But you have an uncanny ability for cheering people up. Apply it, please!"

As they were speaking, Julian West came clumping down the stairs. "Where am I to go?" he asked Lily curtly.

Phoebe took over. "You must be Captain West," she said, approaching him. "How very nice to meet you. I'm Phoebe Twinkle. I live here and work in the village."

She was so sparkling and attractive that West almost smiled. "What work do you do?" he asked, as she took his arm and led him toward the yellow parlor.

"I make hats and do a bit of sewing for people in the village."

This obviously pleased him. "I like young people with initiative," he said. "I believe perhaps that this era will be a turning point where people who use their own skills will prevail as the founders of our country once did. It's not easy, but if you have the self-discipline, nobody can fire you or cut back your hours of gainful work. Which is happening to far too many people these days."

Lily was trailing them along, thinking that Phoebe had already made a conquest. And no wonder she herself hadn't. As far as West knew, Lily and Robert were just part of the idle rich. The mansion seemed to say that. If he only knew . . .

Julian West's entrance created quite a stir. Addie was pouring herself another tiny glass of sherry, which she nearly dropped when he came into the parlor. Lily made a point of introducing Addie to him first even though she knew the 'senior' woman, Mrs. Ethridge, should have had the honor.

Addie was, for once, nearly speechless, and stut-

tered a few words of welcome and said that she'd
read all his books and had really and truly looked
forward to meeting him, but never thought she'd
have a chance, and then her former student had
invited her . . . She suddenly stopped and said,
"I'm babbling. People must often react to you that
way."

West stared at her for a moment and merely said,
"Yes. They sometimes do."

Bud Carpenter had rather suddenly and silently
appeared behind West. "Captain West doesn't often meet the public, ma'am, and considers it a great
pleasure."

West turned on his man and for a second Lily
wondered if he were going to go into a rage and
strike him. But he merely balled his fists, glared at
Carpenter for a moment and said, "My man seems
to think that I can't speak for myself."

*And you probably shouldn't. Not when you're being
rude to my friend*, Lily thought, but Addie didn't
seem to have taken his remark as insulting. She
was still spellbound.

There was a faint stir from the other side of the
room, where Lorna Pratt Ethridge had risen grace-
fully from a comfortable armchair and was approaching. A faint cloud of a light floral perfume
accompanied her.

"Julian," she said softly.

West stared at her.

"Oh, Captain, here's Miss Pratt," Bud Carpenter
said. "Imagine that. Miss Lorna Pratt after all these
years."

West took her hand and chivalrously bent over
it to bestow an almost-kiss. "Dear Lorna, how very
long it's been."

"Be careful, Julian. You'll make everyone think I'm terribly old," she said in her oddly sultry voice.

"Never say it. You are still eighteen in my eyes." Bud Carpenter smiled.

Lily just gawked. Mrs. Ethridge had mentioned once knowing Julian West, but this exchange seemed to indicate that they had known each other *very* well, probably intimately. Or perhaps it was the woman's flirtatious manner when she was attempting to impress a man. If so, Lily could see how she'd snagged Addie's fiancé. And perhaps Julian West felt chivalry was appropriate for a woman nearly his own age.

"I haven't been eighteen for quite a while, Julian. And neither have you," Mrs. Ethridge was saying in a whispery voice as if they were alone. "Do you remember—"

"Excuse me, Captain," Bud Carpenter said. "Would you like me to mix you a drink?"

"No, I'll fix one for myself," he said, and went to the sideboard.

"And Miss Pratt is fond of cherry brandy as you remember," Bud called after him.

"So I am," she said with surprise. "And it's Mrs. Ethridge now, Bud."

"And is Mr. Ethridge with you?" he asked.

"No, I'm a widow."

Lily couldn't figure it out. Sergeant Bud Carpenter was chatting with Mrs. Ethridge as if they were old friends. But he was Julian West's servant. His valet. Probably his butler at West's home. This was very odd. And yet, when she and Robert and the Prinneys dined together at Grace and Favor, their maid Mimi served dinner and ate at the table with them. If she and Robert could change their standards with changing times, so could anyone else, she supposed.

When Julian West had provided Mrs. Ethridge with her cherry brandy, Lily stepped in and forced West to be introduced to Cecil Hoornart, who had been hovering somewhat angrily.

"You must meet another of our guests," Lily said. "Mr. Cecil Hoornart. I'm sure you know of him. He's a critic, a professor and a writer himself of literary biographies. I'm sure you've seen his reviews of your books."

"I think perhaps I have," West said, shaking hands with Cecil, who obviously wasn't carried away with joy at this lukewarm reception.

"I'm sure you'll have a great many things in common to talk about," Lily said, "but I must introduce you to the others first. She led him across the room where Rachel and Raymond were now examining a very old portrait of an early Brewster.

"He looks like a carpenter, all togged out for Sunday services," Raymond was saying just barely loud enough to be heard.

Lily's introduction this time was perfunctory. Who was Raymond Cameron to make snide remarks about her ancestors, even though for all she knew the man in the portrait might have been exactly what Raymond said.

She noticed that Cecil Hoornart was looking neglected, so she sat down beside him, quite upright so he wouldn't get the impression that she'd come for a long talk, just a brief chat. "What inspired you to do a biography of Julian West?" she asked.

Cecil tented his fingers and nodded approval of the question. "I think it was that his early books and later books are so very different. They could have been written by two entirely different men."

Bud Carpenter had approached them and waited patiently for a break in the conversation. "Is there anything I could bring you?" he asked.

Lily and Cecil both politely said no, as Julian West bellowed across the room, "Bud, come here."

Bud excused himself to attend his master.

Lily went on with the conversation. "What do you mean by that?"

"That the early books were written by a Julian West who was a scholar. They were meticulously researched, well written, and informative. But somehow lacking a truly human element except for the main characters. After the Great War, they were written by a Julian West who had been in a war. Still well researched, but gritty and much more violent. Even the minor characters were wracked with fear. They were dirty, they spoke more realistically. Do you see what I mean?"

"Yes, you're quite right. I believe that's exactly why I like the earlier books better," Lily said with a smile as she rose from her chair.

"Many people feel that way," Cecil said. "I like both and enjoy the contrast."

Her first round of hostess duties almost completed, she went back one last time to the entry hall to see if Robert and Mad Henry had returned. Apparently not. The screwdrivers were still on the floor. She picked them up and put them on a side table and took a deep breath. Pretty soon she could break up the party in the yellow parlor and send them all up to dress for dinner.

The initial part of her job was done and it hadn't gone as badly as it might have.

Chapter 8

Dinner the first night went well. Mrs. Prinney had prepared lamb chops so juicy and tender that Lily vaguely wondered about Mrs. P's true relationship with the town butcher and greengrocer. There were crispy, buttery roasted potatoes, tiny succulent peas, a mint sauce she'd shown Lily how to make the previous summer, and a salad that looked like the greens had been hand-raised in a greenhouse. Robert had taken a kerosene lamp to a distant area of the basement of the house and found a superb stash of very fine wines. He came up with four bottles and had to take a bath to get the cobwebs off himself.

The vast dining room table could easily have seated twenty with lots of room and twenty-four with a bit of crowding, but several leaves had been removed to accommodate twelve with intimacy. Though they were evenly divided between men and women, Lily couldn't work out a way to alternate sexes. She, as hostess, had to sit at one end, and Julian, as guest of honor, at the other.

She put place cards for Addie and Phoebe beside Julian West, thinking Addie was the smartest

woman and Phoebe the prettiest. Mr. Prinney was
next to Addie (he would admire her common
sense) and Raymond was next to Phoebe. Rachel
and Lorna were across from each other, beyond
them, Robert and Cecil faced each other. Which left
Mad Henry on Lily's right and Mrs. Prinney on her
left. This was necessary because that end of the table was closest to the kitchen and Mrs. Prinney
could slip in and out of the room unobtrusively if
there were troubles in the kitchen.

Mimi Smith stood on one side of the table, su-
pervising and helping the serving girl they'd hired
for the evening, and Bud Carpenter volunteered to
be temporary butler and take care of seeing that
everyone had wine, spirits or water. Robert had
whispered to Lily as they were being seated that
Bud didn't want to let the Great Man out of his
sight, which accounted for his lowering himself to
serve strangers in an unfamiliar house. Lily wondered if that were true. And if so, why? Sheer de-
votion to his longtime employer?

Trying to make polite conversation with either
Mad Henry or Mrs. Prinney was heavy going. Mrs.
Prinney was watching everyone eat, smiling at
those who were showing appreciation of her feast
and fretting over those who didn't finish their sal-
ads or peas. Mad Henry kept trying to talk to Robert about some kind of telephone wire project. He
seemed utterly unaware that there were rules of
conversation at formal dinner and he was to talk
to his hostess, and when she switched to speaking
to Mrs. Prinney, he could speak with Robert as
everyone 'changed' partners. Robert was ignoring
him entirely, as he was flirting outrageously with
Rachel on the other side of him.

It seemed to be going well. Lily was a skilled hostess—one of her lessons from the old days when they'd been wealthy and such talents were important on an almost daily basis. Julian West was having a pleasant conversation with Phoebe, seemingly on the values of the working class. Mr. Prinney and Addie were talking about the difference in public and private school education from what snips of conversation Lily caught. Raymond and Lorna Ethridge seemed to have a number of family acquaintances in common and were chattering with animation about the troubles some family named Higginbotham had while last traveling in Europe. Even Cecil Hoornart seemed happy. Next to books and authors, his primary interest in life was food, and when he praised Mrs. Prinney for her menu planning, he got her full attention.

But when Lily turned to Mrs. Prinney and the rest obediently turned to the guest on their other side, it didn't work out quite as well. Mr. Prinney had nothing in common with Rachel. Nor did Julian seem to be enjoying Addie's conversational gambits. Raymond seemed to like looking at Phoebe—what man wouldn't?—but apparently couldn't think of anything to say to her. They were listlessly discussing the weather. Cecil made a hearty attempt to talk about recent books with Lorna, who said she wasn't much of a reader, except, of course, for Julian West's books, which she really didn't like all that much, but felt obligated to buy since she and Julian had known each other for ages and ages and she kept thinking he might base a character on her someday. She said she thought she might have been his model for Dolley Madison in that one book . . . what was the title?

When dessert finally arrived—a wonderful Dutch pastry with raspberries and cream over it—Lily was relieved to turn the conversation one last time.

"Henry, what are you and Robert talking about? I heard you mention telephones."

"I'm going to install a system to replace your bells," Henry said. "I've looked over your system and they're all quite taut and the new wire will thread along them nicely."

"And what will that accomplish?" Lily asked, trying to speak to him while eavesdropping on the rest of the conversations.

"Instead of a guest having to ring a bell in his room that chimes in the servants' kitchen in the basement, and possibly someone who isn't the right person coming to the room, don't you see, the guest can actually say what they need or ask a question and get the right person."

"Oh, I see. I think," Lily said. "This doesn't involve any new wiring, does it? Remember . . ."

"No, no, I'll just run telephone wire along the bell pull wires that are here already. And very small sound producers in the rooms. If you like it, they'll be put into the walls—"

"Oh, no! You and Robert are not going to tear holes in walls while we have company in the house."

Mad Henry laughed merrily. "No, they can just sit on the floor for now."

"Very well, but don't disturb anyone doing this, please."

What a very silly idea, Lily thought, but Mad Henry was full of silly ideas and this one sounded relatively harmless.

As dessert was being consumed (only Rachel, watching her figure, declining this treat) table talk was allowed to become general. Cecil spoke rather loudly to Julian West. "How did you come to be in the army in the Great War, sir? I understand you weren't a military man before then. Not in the sense of serving in the army, if I recall correctly."

Julian looked at him for a long moment, as if trying to remember who Cecil was, and then said, "Oh, you're the book review chap—"

"And your biographer, sir."

West gave Cecil another long, blank stare and finally said, "I had studied for the ministry in my youth. I'm afraid I lost my faith about the same time I completed my studies. But I did have a degree, and they needed chaplains over there. It qualified me as an officer, like doctors and technical specialists.

"But I didn't want to parade myself as a false chaplain, so I contacted a gentleman named Newton Baker who had written to me three years earlier, complimenting my books for their accuracy. A man who had become U. S. Secretary of War in the meantime. He had the power to give me any rank he wanted and any help I wanted to get to the front. And I was to send him reports that he believed I could do without bias. I did have six weeks of basic training before they sent me off to the Argonne Forest."

At the words "Argonne Forest," most of the table fell silent. They were two of the most ominous words in the world for those who had lived through the Great War as adults.

Cecil Hoornart, however, was respectful but undeterred. "I wonder, sir, if you could tell us about your personal experience in the war?"

"I suppose so. But the ladies wouldn't like it, and certainly not over such a fine meal as we've all had."

Lily glanced at Bud Carpenter, holding a bottle of brandy and frowning. What had he to look unhappy about?

Lorna spoke up. "I for one remember the Great War vividly. I lost two brothers, one in Belgium, one in France. I would like to hear your account. I'm not a silly, fainting girl anymore."

"Nor am I," Addie said.

Rachel said nothing, but Lily felt obliged, as hostess, to say, "I would very much like to hear a firsthand account." Which wasn't true, but was her duty, she felt.

The ladies left the table first and headed off to freshen lipstick and visit their various bathrooms. Phoebe descended the steps from her third floor room at the same time Lily started down from the second floor.

"Mr. West seems quite taken with you, Phoebe," Lily said.

"He's just slumming," Phoebe said cheerfully. "All that nonsense about the downtrodden working class. I haven't the heart to tell him I consider myself an artist, or at least a craftswoman. I'm not really looking forward to hearing all about the Great War either."

"Nor am I, but I must endure it. You needn't," Lily said. "Just sit a bit out of his sight and slip out the nearest door. Or I could make up a headache for you right now."

"I can probably take it," Phoebe said.

Addie was already in the parlor, having run a wet brush through her wild hair. And Rachel arrived a moment after Lily and Phoebe. Mrs. Prinney ran in briefly to tell Lily she felt she must wash the crystal herself rather than trusting the hired kitchen help and would try to get back later although she didn't really want to hear war stories.

"No, please don't bother to come back," Lily said. "You've worked yourself to the bone already and you need your rest. If you get one of your headaches, we'll all go down in flames."

Lily poured the women tiny glasses of sherry and they chatted amiably about what a nice dinner it had been. Rachel mentioned how they'd been stopped along Route 9 to have the car searched because of the Lindbergh baby.

"The papers said there were a man's footprints to the house and the ladder both coming and going and a woman's footprints along with the man's well away from the house. I'm a little insulted, however, that anybody could have thought that Raymond and I looked like the sort of people who would steal a baby, for heaven's sake!"

Lily barely managed to refrain from asking what people who would steal a baby could be expected to look like.

Lorna was the last to arrive and looked ravishing. She'd added a bit of jewelry to her ensemble and refreshed her floral perfume.

The men, having presumably fulfilled their duty of having a glass of port and some manly talk in a very short time, joined the ladies only moments after Lorna arrived.

Julian West took a position by the fireplace

warming his hands. Everybody settled in to listen to his account.

For a virtual hermit, he had a stunning delivery. When the room was quiet, he turned and said, dramatically, "The thing I remember most about the war was the smell. We don't often notice odors except in passing, but the stench of the war is with me now and probably will haunt me the rest of my life. It was a porridge of death and decay and foul mud."

I'm not going to like this, Lily thought.

Julian West, having delivered this line, went back in time. "I'd followed the progress of the war in the newspapers and was astonished at the sheer idiocy of it. As a writer who studied wars, I knew this was the most ill-founded and badly led of all. But when America got into it, I thought it would change, in spite of my own training, which was useless and tedious. All very impractical quick marches, slow marches, hand signals everyone had to learn, silly rules about filling in garbage dumps and latrines before moving forward. As if warriors have all the time in the world for housekeeping.

"There had been no military tactics whatsoever. The French and English had simply been sending wave after wave of young men over the top of the trenches to be slaughtered. And so had the Germans. I foolishly thought when the Americans went in, real warfare would finish it off. As a patriot, I thought our generals would be smarter, more experienced and would have a genuine sense of military maneuvers designed to win, rather than sending helpless young men to be machine gunned."

Julian took a sip of his drink and went on. "I

joined up and my cousin John, who had been my secretary, best friend, and student, insisted on joining up with me. So did our man Bud Carpenter. As a nominal chaplain, I was able to convince the authorities that I needed both of them with me. We had six weeks of training, as I said earlier, just a lot of useless marching in step, then took a ship to St. Navarre where Black Jack Pershing had landed the American Expeditionary Forces initially.

"We rode in crowded trucks across France to the southwest. As we approached the Argonne Forest, we could hear and smell the war. At first only faintly. But soon the sound and stench became overwhelming. At one point, I was riding in the front with the driver and as we came over a low rise, I could see the forest of Argonne. But it was no longer a forest. It was a landscape of miles of fallen or denuded trees and craters and mud. It was as if long dead trees had been dumped on the moon or Mars.

"In civilian life we think of trenches as long, clean cuts in the earth for laying pipes. But in wars, the trenches are zig-zagged. This is so that the enemy can't drop down into a trench and kill a line of men with a few efficient shots. With the zig-zag, he could only get the few in one leg of the trench, and would have no idea what was around the next corner coming at him.

"These trenches had utterly destroyed the landscape. Vast amounts of boggy soil had been laboriously dug up and piled in front of the trenches as parapets. Communication trenches ran through as supply lines and for removal of bodies and injured men being taken back."

Julian West was so absorbed in what he was saying that he didn't seem to notice Phoebe Twinkle go pale and slip out the door. Lorna Pratt Ethridge was leaning a bit forward in her chair, as if not wanting to miss a word.

Rachel, who had claimed not to be a sissy, was looking down and twisting her hands in her lap.

Even Cecil looked a bit queasy.

The account got worse.

Chapter 9

"I thought my first view of the battlefield was the most awful thing I'd ever seen," Julian West said. "Until we got closer. Until I spent cold night after night sleeping in a slimy ooze of blood, rotting flesh, bloated rats gorging themselves on the dead and dying and running over the living as if we were no more than part of the landscape.

"We slept through barrages of gunfire and bombs and the screams of men. We didn't dare let our gas masks get lost. Clouds of greasy, foul mustard gas would drift over no-man's-land. We could hear the wounded men out there who hadn't been rescued and wouldn't be until dark, coughing before we even saw the gas cloud.

"Mustard gas is heavier than air and it would slither over any parapet that wasn't high enough and lie in a miasma around us. Even now, and probably for decades to come, possibly to the end of this century, it remains in the soil. And a man who wants to reclaim the ruined land for farming can plow into a trench and die horribly as a result of releasing the fumes.

"The Tommys and Frogs who had survived the

earlier years were wily men, but our poor young doughboys hadn't been told what deadly forces they were up against. All they'd been told was how to march in order, and understand hand signals, and to stay away from loose foreign women in the cities.

"The first day John, Bud and I were in the trenches, four of the youngsters were playing cards when a mustard gas cannister landed in our section of trench and exploded. By the time they could find their gas masks, they were coughing up bloody foam and pieces of their lungs."

Almost nobody could meet anyone else's gaze. Only Lily and Robert looked directly at each other. Robert's face was frigid and white. Should there be another war after the War to End All Wars, which was inevitable given human nature, he might confront something like this.

It was too horrible to contemplate and Lily wished she'd left the room with Phoebe. She had an eerie feeling, too, that Julian West was, in some perverse way, showing off. He was enjoying making them heartsick. But wasn't that part of the job of the wordsmith?

Julian went on "Oddly enough, another thing that I remember most vividly was the lack of color. The ground was a soupy gray-brown. Our uniforms quickly turned the same color. The sky, always filled with smoke, was gray-brown. I never saw a clear blue sky. The standing trunks and few limbs of trees were leafless and pitted with holes and were brown. Some had bits of bone and flesh stuck to them. There were no toilets, only holes in the ground back behind the lines, and the boys with cholera couldn't get there. Their shit was brown. The rats were brown. Only the blood was red, and it soon turned brown. Oh, and the orange-brown slugs that one was always accidentally putting one's hand on. We couldn't bathe. We had lice in our hair and underwear. Most of the men got trench foot, some of them lost their feet to it when the gangrene set in."

Somebody made a faint gagging noise. Rachel stood up suddenly and left the room. Bud Carpenter was standing by the door to the room and opened the door for her with a perfectly blank expression on his face.

Cecil, apparently having had enough of the gruesome details, asked a question. "How long were you there?"

"Two months. Two years, two decades, it seemed," West said. "It seemed a lifetime. I was afraid I'd never see another flat field of healthy crops or a house that was intact or a church that hadn't been bombed to rumble. Or another pretty girl in a clean dress or decent food on a white plate, or birds. I'd make myself imagine such things to put myself to sleep, trying to block out the sound of rats squeaking and gnawing. Such common things we thought about just to keep our sanity and survive, but they are gone now along a wide strip of devastation from Belgium clear to Switzerland."

He paused to sip the last of his drink. Robert silently took the glass from him and refilled it.

"Thank you," West said, then continued, "I wondered often where the people who had lived there for generations had gone. They'd survived the onslaught of ancient Romans and Mongols and Huns, the constant small wars on the border of France and Germany, the Napoleonic wars, and somehow kept their farms and forests, but not this war."

He took a deep draught of his drink and coughed slightly.

"The land was ruined, the forest was dead, fouled for all time with death. Row after row of stinking trenches marking the ebb and flow of armies pushing each other back and forth at the points of bayonets."

West set his drink on the mantel and lit a cigarette, flipping the wooden match into the fireplace. He took a long draw on the cigarette and went on. "Unexploded bombs were left behind in trenches, waiting to kill the unwary for decades to come, bodies and parts of bodies were squashed into the mud where someday if you ever tried to dig a basement you'd be bound to come across the twisted, crushed remains."

It was obvious that Cecil had failed to turn the tide of the narrative. He tried again. "Was the war over while you were there? Is that why you left in two months?"

"No, it wasn't over. I was responsible for the dying men. And the dead. John and Bud and I would accompany them back behind the Western Front. Trucks full of dead and dying alongside each other. Sometimes they were all dead before we got them to the hospital tents. I'd leave them either to the medics or the burial details and we'd go back to the front for more. That sounds like an easy job, I know. Hard on the heart, but easy.

"Not so. The roads were narrow, constantly clogged with trucks that were trying to get food, and ammunition, and yet more stupid, innocent young men to the front. We'd have to stop and lay our dead in the mud to lighten the weight of our vehicles so we wouldn't sink into the mess as well while we helped push the trucks out of ruts. Bud would sit with them to keep the rats away while my cousin and I pushed trucks."

Lily glanced at Bud. He was absolutely expressionless, but was nodding slightly.

"About six weeks in, one of our boys found a wooden chair in a deserted farmhouse and it was the only luxury we had. They had a roster of who got to sit in a real chair for an hour. In the middle of the night some months later, the Fritz lobbed something highly incendiary over the parapet and set the chair on fire and killed the boy sitting on it. The burning chair made a beacon, a target. We had to put the fire out. My cousin ran to throw a blanket over it to smother the flame."

West drew a long breath and squashed out his cigarette in a ashtray stand next to the fireplace. "It must have been the only dry blanket in the whole army. Or maybe it had come into contact with a leaking petrol can from a truck. I never knew. It burst into flames. I pulled him away and pummeled him with my hands to put out the flames—"

He gestured feebly at his face and spread his hands. "I got this, but my cousin died in agony. His flesh was charred over so much of his body that he went into shock. Bud and I took his body back ourselves to the mortuary tent. It wasn't until we got to the medic tent that I had any idea how badly I was burned as well."

"And you were sent back home?" Cecil asked. His voice was shaky.

"Not home. Only to England. I spent six months having surgery and treatment. I didn't care so much about my face, but my fingers had to work or I couldn't ever write again."

He knocked back the last of his drink and subsided onto the arm of a sofa near the fireplace.

"Bud stayed with me over everybody's objections. When we finally returned to New York, I threw away my suitcase, saving only my notes, copies of the letters I'd sent Newton Baker, and a partial manuscript I'd worked on. And even that was in a sealed, waxed container so I didn't have to smell it. Bud went out and got us new clothes and we threw away our uniforms, which the hospital had insisted we had to wear on the boat home. I couldn't stand the smell.

"When we finally got upstate, it was warm weather. I opened the sealed package outdoors and copied everything to fresh, clean paper in the breeze and burned the originals, which stank of death and rank mud. Or perhaps the smell was only locked in my brain."

He looked around the room. "Sometimes I dream that smell and wake up gagging. Sometimes I imagine I get a faint whiff of it even when waking. The worst smell in the world's history."

There was a collective sigh, but no one spoke. West finally said, "Aren't you sorry you asked?"

Lorna Ethridge spoke up for the first time since West had started talking. "No, we need to know. Everyone needs to know. So it won't ever happen again."

"Oh, it'll happen again," West said. "The War to End All Wars is an immoral phrase. The Germans are grudge-holders. Just a few months ago, they refused to pay any more war reparation money. And if the crazy house painter Adolf Hitler should win in the next election, there *will* be another war.

"And then there's the Pope being a fool," he said angrily. "Last December the 'Vicar of Christ'—God's peacemaker—refused to meet with Gandhi—a true peacemaker—because of the way Gandhi dressed, for God's sake! And two months later, he's being chummy with Mussolini, who is a bully and a thug. Without a positive influence from the leader of the biggest, most powerful religious organization in Europe and America, how could we have peace? Oh, yes. There will be another Great War.

"But I hope it doesn't start again before the American military realizes that just sending the flower of our youth out into no-man's-land and telling them to march in neat tidy lines is a lunatic way of killing them. I don't think the public will ever know what an idiotic, haphazard war this one was."

He glanced at his watch. "It's late. And I've taken up your whole evening. I won't wish you sweet dreams."

He rose and left the room, Bud Carpenter following in his wake.

Lily glanced around and realized for the first time that Mad Henry hadn't been there at all that she'd noticed. Everyone else remained nearly silent, drifting off to their rooms one by one, stunned by what they'd heard. A few goodnights were said in dull tones.

Lily moved over to the sofa and sat staring at the fire. She'd been only seven years old when the Great War started and eleven when it ended. All she remembered of it was when a distant British cousin had died and there had been a memorial service for him at the family church in New York. She'd never met him, was bored and fidgety. But now she was deeply saddened to know that one of her own—one of the flowers of youth West spoke of—had died a probably horrible death.

She nearly jumped out of her skin when a hand fell lightly on her shoulder. She whirled and saw that it was Lorna Ethridge. Lily had thought she was alone in the room.

"I'm sorry to interrupt your thoughts. Which are no doubt quite dour at the moment, but I wanted a private word with you."

A private chat right now was the last thing in the world Lily wanted, but she said, "So long as it's not about the war."

"No, but a different war of sorts. Addie Jonson is being quite cold and remote to me. I thought she understood and had forgotten and forgiven."

She paused, waiting for Lily to comment, but Lily said nothing.

"I suppose she's told you about her relationship with my late husband."

"A little," Lily said. "It's really none of my business."

"But if she's told you her view, I feel obligated to tell you the truth of the matter."

The fire had burned quite low now and a small log cracked and rolled toward the front of the fireplace. Lily got up to push it back and make sure no sparks had gotten to the rug.

"You see, I really rescued Anthony from her," Lorna said to Lily's back. "I knew poor Addie had no idea of his true feelings. She's the dearest girl in the world. The dearest woman now, but still a girl then in her thinking. Anthony had been wounded in the war. Did she tell you that?"

Lily merely nodded and brushed at the rug once more. Then turned and sat down on it. She didn't want to share the sofa with Mrs. Ethridge.

"He'd allowed himself to become far more helpless than he really was. And it was his very helplessness that appealed to a young, healthy woman on the brink of spinsterhood who probably was longing for marriage, if not children. It was she who had suggested their engagement. Anthony admitted to me that he was half frightened of her youth and energy and determination to pretend they were young lovers."

Lorna stood and delicately wrung her hands. "I suppose, in some way, I felt a similar sense of wanting to save him from himself. But I knew he couldn't be treated as an invalid or he would be one the rest of his life, however long or short it might be. I tried to 'buck him up,' as they say. He liked being treated like a man, a mature man, but still a man. And we had so much more in common."

"I suppose so," Lily said quietly when Lorna again paused for an obligatory reaction.

"We were roughly of an age, Anthony and I. We loved travel. We cared nothing about children and the details of their education, both being childless ourselves. Aside from Anthony, it was the only thing Addie cared deeply about. That, and keeping her various properties in good shape, which was also quite boring to Anthony and me. I don't doubt that she imagined herself madly in love with him— but it was an illusion. They had nothing to talk about. Anthony said she didn't even care about good food, which he and I appreciated enormously. He was quite an excellent cook and so was I at the time, although I've given it up now."

Lily was desperate to escape this performance, which she felt had an air of very careful rehearsal about it. She felt she was betraying Addie to even allow herself to hear it.

"I'm sorry for all of you. It must have been horrible," Lily said, getting up and putting the fire screen back and making as if she were heading for the door.

"Please wait just a moment. I just want you to know that I loved Anthony as much as your friend Addie imagined she loved him. I'm really not an ogre and I wouldn't want you to think so."

Lily felt she'd been pushed to the brink. "Then why did you tell me Addie had spoken to you about this house party?"

"But she had!" Lorna exclaimed. "I—I think she was speaking to me anyway. It was at a city hall meeting that a friend had dragged me to. Something about zoning. Too boring for words, but my friend needed a lift in my car, and I decided to sit it out. Afterward, a group of women who knew each other were talking and Addie glanced toward me several times as she spoke about how anxious she was to meet Julian West in person."

"Did you specifically invite you to contact me?"

Lorna had the grace to look ever so slightly embarrassed. "Not in so many words, but she had mentioned your name and where the party was to be held and she knew that I had once been acquainted with Julian. She said something like, 'I guess you'd like to renew that acquaintance.' And I assumed she was being sarcastic, but later convinced myself she was sincere. I've never known

Addie to use sarcasm, you see. She's so admirably straightforward in her speech. It must come from being a teacher, I suppose."

Lily rubbed her eyes. "Mrs. Ethridge, I'm sorry, but I must really check on Mrs. Prinney's plans for tomorrow and I'm very tired."

At that, Mrs. Ethridge hugged Lily warmly and said, "I didn't mean to impose. Really I didn't. I really just hoped"—she shrugged elegantly—"that we could be friends, too."

Lily managed a faint smile. "Good night," she said. And forced herself to walk away slowly rather than to obviously flee.

When Lily reached the door, Bud Carpenter opened it for her. It wasn't until she'd gotten to her room that she realized that he'd left with Julian West earlier. When had he come back to the yellow parlor?

And why? He'd obviously overheard the whole conversation with Lorna as he stood silently in the semidarkness by the door. Was that his purpose in returning to the room?

Chapter 10

Robert went to the kitchen to find something to nibble. He'd been so busy talking to the guests during dinner that he hadn't eaten much. And while Julian West's talk had been a stomach-churner, nothing could really override his appetite.

He rummaged in the ice box and found a leftover dessert. The one Rachel hadn't wanted. As he was nearly finished, he heard an odd noise. He abandoned the last crumbs of his snack and went down the pantry steps to the servants' kitchen and sitting room, which was in the finished part of the basement under the family kitchen. It hadn't been used for many years, but Mimi the housekeeper, who was obsessed with cleanliness, kept it spotless anyway.

Mad Henry was there in a snarl of wires, for this was where the previously used bell pull system had been centered in the distant past.

"Henry, it's quite late," Robert said.

"I've almost got it working, I think. Hold this," he said, handing a wire to Robert.

"You've put the things in the upstairs rooms already? In one evening?"

"I was sorry to miss the talk, but it was a perfect time. Everybody else was in the parlor, so I could work without bothering anybody. Except for Miss Twinkle coming up early. And I'd already done her room."

Henry hooked up the wire Robert was holding to another he'd been twisting and said, "That ought to do it."

"You test it out yourself. I'm giving up for the day," Robert said, yawning. He found most of Mad Henry's projects interesting, but this one didn't grab his imagination. It might have been the practical device he'd always thought Mad Henry might come up with, but as no one but Mimi ever came down here, and then only to tidy things up, it was of no use to Grace and Favor.

Lily had gone to her room, prepared for bed and picked up the book she'd been reading. But she couldn't even remember where she'd left off. She read a few random pages that didn't seem familiar. She had too much else on her mind.

Julian West's talk, of course, was uppermost in her thoughts. It had been so vivid that she was half afraid to go to sleep for fear she'd dream she was in the war.

The other thing jostling around in her mind, and giving her even more personal trouble, was the conversation with Lorna Ethridge. Lily's loyalty was entirely to Addie, but Lorna spun a good story. It might be true. It fit with Addie's personality. Addie took her enthusiasms seriously.

Anthony Ethridge, apparently a milksop of the first order, might well have let Addie convince him that they were to marry, then got frightened of the consequences. And, as an older man, he might have felt much more attraction to Lorna than to Addie. If Lorna was telling the truth, she would have been a better life-companion to him, sharing his interests more than Addie ever could. Besides, Lorna was a beautiful woman. Addie, unfortunately, wasn't.

But the account of how Addie "invited" Lorna to Grace and Favor was very thin. Lily didn't believe that for a moment. Addie had been appalled that Lorna had turned up at Grace and Favor and clearly had not intended to invite her. In fact, Addie had mentioned, Lily thought, that she hadn't even spoken to Lorna Ethridge for years even though they lived in the same town. So if Lorna Ethridge was lying about that, as she obviously was, why should Lily believe her other story?

Lily set her book aside, turned out her light and brooded. She was almost asleep when she heard a scratching noise. She flung off the covers and went to the door, thinking that someone was trying to get her attention in a terribly subtle manner. Nobody was there, but the scratchy noise continued. Why wasn't Agatha barking her head off about it? It was coming from somewhere in her room.

Turning the light back on and moving her head this way and that, she traced the sound to the chair by the bathroom door. Was there a creature under the chair? Had she a weapon to fend it off? She backed away a bit, leaned down and took a cautious look. There was nothing under the chair but a little wooden box with a black circle in the middle. She eased forward, picked up the box and listened. It was static she'd heard.

Mad Henry!

She threw on a robe and went to hunt him down. It took quite a while, but she eventually located him in the servants' basement.

"Henry, what are you doing?"

"Testing out my invention, of course," Mad Henry said in a somewhat patronizing tone.

"Well, you're making an irritating noise in my room and probably others as well. Please turn it off and play around with it in the morning."

Mad Henry put his hands up. "Five more minutes. That's all."

Lily stomped off and went back upstairs. The second floor had only one light on in the hallway and it appeared that the light bulb had gone out while she was down in the basement talking to Henry. There was no illumination but a shred of moonlight from a window at the end of the hall. She'd have to feel her way to her room. As she moved along blindly, a door along the hall somewhere opened and closed quietly. *Who was roaming around?* she wondered.

Entering her room, Lily discovered that the scratchy noise had been replaced with the faint sound of music being played. Henry had apparently hooked his system up to a radio. Suddenly the sound was cut off and there was a blissful silence. Except for the sound of another door somewhere down the hall being opened and closed.

In the morning, most of the guests turned up for breakfast. Lily had placed little lists on the bedside tables of all the rooms, indicating what time meals were planned and other activities were available. This evening there was another dinner with several people from the town. Dr. Polhemus, Jack Summer

and the new police chief would be there, and
bridge and pachisi were planned for after dinner.

There was to be a walk this morning along the
paths that wound between the houses on the hill
and the one that led down to Voorburg. It was a
beautiful day for a leisurely walk. Spring wild
flowers were blooming along the sides of the road
and in the forest the paths went through.

"Are you going on the walk with me?" she asked
as Addie entered the dining room.

"I'd love that. It's such nice weather," Addie
said, looking over the array of breakfast food on
the long table on the inside wall. She chose kip-
pered herring, scrambled eggs, one of Mrs. Prinney's marvelous pastries and orange juice, and sat
down between Robert and Lily.

"How about if I offer to take people to town in
the Duessie?" Robert asked.

"Is there a dress shop?" Rachel asked over the
oatmeal she was picking through for the raisins.

"I'm afraid there isn't," Lily said. "There was
once, but it's gone out of business. Like so many
small businesses around the country."

"I've noticed that," Rachel said, sounding perplexed about this inconvenient trend. "I'll ride
along with Robert anyway. I like quaint little towns
and Raymond wouldn't let us stop and look it over
on the way."

"You didn't ask me to," Raymond replied from
the other end of the table. "And I didn't want us
to be late, especially after we got tied up in the
traffic check." He shifted his gaze to Lily. "That
was quite an impressive talk last night, wasn't it?
Not exactly what I'd expected, but fascinating."

"It was appalling," Rachel said. "I can't imagine

why people want to know the gory details of a war. It was disgusting."

"Rachel, you have your head in the sand," Raymond said. "As usual. Wars are important. They shape our history. I wouldn't be surprised if this economic crisis the world is in now is an indirect result of the Great War in some way. And the worldwide depression may lead to another, as West suggested."

"You must ask Mr. West about that," Lily suggested.

"Ask Mr. West about what?" Cecil Hoornart said as he entered the room. "Is he coming down for breakfast?"

Lily explained what the question was and added, "I don't know if he's breakfasting. I didn't ask anyone last night, though I meant to."

Cecil had filled his plate with generous portions of everything and sat down eyeing it all before choosing to start with the scone. "Umm, wonderful," he said. "Your Mrs. Prinney is to be congratulated. Too many people get scones either rock hard or soggy. But these are perfection."

Julian West, looking very tired and irritable, came into the dining room with Bud Carpenter following. West sat at the head of the table, nodded curtly to the others while Bud served him black coffee and two pieces of toast.

"Is that all you want, sir?" Robert asked. "There's all sorts of good stuff on the buffet."

Bud replied, "The Captain eats sparsely in the morning so as to not interfere with his writing."

Whether this was merely an explanatory remark or an order was hard to determine. It sounded more like an order in Carpenter's gruff voice. Lily wondered how Mr. West tolerated the man. But then she thought back to his talk last night, which featured Sergeant Bud Carpenter as a loyal man who had followed his employer to the very heart of a terrible war. She supposed this had tied them together in some way for life. You couldn't endure what they had endured together and just walk away from that kind of loyalty.

Phoebe, on her way to work, dropped in and made an egg sandwich to eat as she walked down the path to town. "I'm sorry to miss your plans, but I have to go to work. Mrs. Roosevelt is coming in this morning to pick up a hat."

"Which Mrs. Roosevelt?" Cecil asked.

"Mrs. Eleanor, the Governor's wife," Phoebe said, wrapping her sandwich in a napkin.

"You make hats for Eleanor Roosevelt?" Julian West asked, surprised.

"Terrible hats, I'm afraid," Phoebe said with a laugh. "She's a dear woman, but has no taste in hats. I've tried to get her into more flattering ones, but she says she'd feel like a homely peacock in a pretty hat. I'll see all of you later."

"I'd forgotten that the Governor lived so close to you," Julian West said. "Do you see him often?"

"Only sometimes through a window of his train," Lily said. "It picks him up at Hyde Park, and Voorburg is a few stops along the line."

"I'm glad he's running for President," West said.

"You don't think he could possibly win, do you?" Raymond said in a shocked voice.

"I'm sure he will. Who would vote for Hoover after the mess he's made of this country?"

"I don't think you can blame Hoover for what's happened. He's a good man," Raymond objected.

"He was in charge of supplying badly needed nourishing food to the Europeans after the Great War."

"And he's letting his own people starve," West said with finality.

"But Roosevelt is a Democrat," Raymond persisted.

"Not having the benefit of growing up as you have in the upper strata of society, I'm at liberty to vote for the best candidate," West said.

That silenced Raymond.

"Who's going for a walk with me?" Lily said with nearly hysterical chirpiness.

Only Addie took her up on the offer. Cecil intended to come, but when he went up to his room to change into his hiking clothes, he discovered that his manuscript was missing. He was frantic and tried to rouse everyone to mount a thorough search.

When he came back to report this to Lily, Addie said, "You've just put it down somewhere and forgotten. Calm down and think rationally when you last saw it. Taking a walk with us will clear your head."

Julian West had said he had work to do. Raymond and Rachel went for a ride to town with Robert. It wasn't until Lily and Addie were setting out for their walk that Lily said, "I haven't seen Lorna Ethridge this morning."

"I didn't hear her stirring," Addie said. "I imagine she's the sort of woman who sleeps late in the morning."

Cecil, who was interested enough in gossip to forget his manuscript for a moment, said, "That sounds like a criticism. Don't you like Mrs. Ethridge?"

"I despise her, as a matter of fact," Addie said. "But I can avoid her quite nicely in a big house like Grace and Favor. Oh, what a lovely little daffodil. Did you plant these, Lily?"

"No, they're wild. Or someone planted them years ago."

Cecil took the hint that Lorna was a forbidden subject. "How long have you and your brother lived here, Miss Brewster?"

"Only since last August, and you must call me Lily. We inherited the house from our great-uncle. My brother and I have never lived in a rural setting before, except in the summers when we stayed in the family beach house in Massachusetts for a couple weeks and occasional autumn visits to our house in North Carolina. I've come to enjoy it quite a bit, but Robert's having a little more trouble with it. He's a city person. He misses the night life."

Cecil said, "I wouldn't. I'm an early to bed, early to rise person. I do my best work in the mornings. I did oversleep a bit today, however. There was an odd noise in my room and several people seemed to be roaming around in the halls and slamming doors."

"I noticed that, too," Lily said. "The strange noise in your room was caused by Mad Henry. He's apparently replaced the bell pull wires with telephone wires to make a calling system. Of course, no one is ever in the basement servants' quarters to answer either the call or the bell pulls. But he means well, I suppose."

Addie picked a tiny red tulip and stuck it in the buttonhole of her shirt. "What is the manuscript you're working on now, Professor Hoornart? Another book of your reviews? I enjoyed the last one very much and added a great many books to my reading list on your recommendations."

Cecil stood up a little straighter and smiled benevolently. "I'm glad to hear that. But no, my current project is another biography. Of Mr. Julian West, in fact. Which is why I was so very glad to be invited here. But I'm worried about my manuscript and notes. I had them just last night."

"It must not be easy to do a biography of Julian West," Lily said. "I understand he's a very solitary person and never gives interviews. I was very surprised that he accepted our invitation."

"Interviews aren't really the most important thing," Cecil said. "I'm really examining the body of his work. One can't help but reveal one's true nature when one is a writer. Especially a writer of historical fiction. One's changing views of life creep into the work."

"And how do you think his work has changed?" Addie asked.

"I presume you've read all his work, Miss Jonson? The early works were more balanced. Not more cheerful, exactly, but they had a sense of irony that was often somewhat amusing in spots. More even-handed. His work after the war is missing that. The irony is bitter, the views are bleak. It's a significant change, and well it should be. After hearing all he said last night, I can see quite well what caused the difference in style. I was talking about it last evening with Lily."

"I suppose you'd change enormously after a horrible experience like that," Lily said. "The sheer brutality . . ."

"I believe a great many men who survived that war were severely altered," Cecil said. "My cousin had a husband who suffered shell-shock. He's never gotten over it. His wife left him because he couldn't talk about anything but the war and had horrible nightmares and would wake screaming almost every night. He'd been a very mild, interesting and pleasant person before. He became a frightening stranger to her."

"And I understand many of the young men came home with serious drinking problems as well," Addie said. "I had a madly teetotaler uncle in the war who came home a permanent drunk and eventually died of alcohol poison."

"I've heard that, too. What a pity," Cecil said.

Lily wasn't quite ready for another round of depressing talk. "I wonder," she said desperately, "if it's possible to press some of these spring flowers. I'm not sure what you'd do with them when they were dried, but it would be a nice reminder of spring."

Neither Cecil nor Addie had any comment on this vapid subject. Cecil wasn't really paying attention either. "I remember putting the manuscript and notes on the table under the window in my room. I'm sure that was where I put it."

"Perhaps you moved it later," Lily suggested. "And you've forgotten where. I'm sure if you stop worrying about it, you'll remember where you put it sooner or later. Don't you find that sometimes if you *don't* think about something, it just comes to your mind later?"

Cecil stared at Lily, uncomprehending. "I have to get back to the house," he said. "Perhaps I put it on the lower shelf of the table and just forgot to look. Or possibly your maid put it away in a drawer while I was at breakfast."

He was sounding more alarmed by the minute. "Or maybe someone took it on purpose," he added.

"Oh, surely not," Addie said. "I'm always misplacing things and later finding them exactly where I thought they were and already looked. I'm sure it's in your room." Changing the subject, she asked Lily, "Is this village party tomorrow or Sunday?" Addie asked. "I'm looking forward to it."

Lily watched Cecil hurrying away and answered in a preoccupied manner, "It's on Saturday. It'll be nice according to Mrs. Prinney."

Somehow she couldn't imagine Cecil misplacing something as important as his manuscript and notes. She wished he'd safely stashed it in Mr. Prinney's safe. But it was silly to think someone had taken it. Who would want to?

Chapter 11

When Lily and Addie arrived back at the mansion, Phoebe Twinkle was waiting for them. Her face was flushed from rapidly walking up the hill. "Mrs. Roosevelt came in for her hat this morning, Lily, and while she was trying it on, I told her about your guest. I hope you don't mind. She was so excited to hear it." Phoebe leaned over slightly, to catch her breath. "And she said that the Governor had read all his books and would love to meet him. We've all been invited to Hyde Park tomorrow."

"All of us?" Lily exclaimed.

"Any of the party who wishes to go."

"Unless Julian West doesn't want to go."

"Oh, yes. I guess that's right."

"It's almost time for luncheon. I'll ask him then. Can you stop and eat, Phoebe?"

"No, I have to get back to the shop. I'd have called, but I don't have a telephone at the shop and the butcher was using his. So I must rush away."

Lily realized as Phoebe dashed off, that the village party was tomorrow. She and Robert would have to be present, at least as nominal hosts, even though the people of Voorburg set it all up themselves and needed nothing but access to bathrooms.

Robert, Raymond and Rachel arrived home from their jaunt while Phoebe was leaving. Though Robert offered her a ride back to town, she said, "The uphill part is when I could have used a ride. Downhill is a breeze."

Lily signaled to Robert to wait while Raymond and Rachel went indoors to freshen up for luncheon. "Robert, such news! We've all been invited to meet the Governor tomorrow."

"Any particular governor?"

"Roosevelt, of course. Mrs. Roosevelt was at Phoebe's today picking up a hat and Phoebe told her about Julian West being here, and Mrs. Roosevelt invited all of us for a visit."

"That's just the giraffe's neck!" Robert exclaimed. "Wait till I tell my friends. I'll turn it into a private dinner, of course, and not mention West at all when I dine out on the story."

Lily smiled briefly. "The only problem would be if West refuses the invitation. Then none of us could go. He's the reason for the visit. And one of us has to stay here and be on hand for the village party."

"Leave West to me, Lily. He expressed a bias toward the Governor. I think he'll drool at the chance to meet him. And I don't see why you couldn't slip away for an hour. Maybe two. The village fête goes on all day."

Gradually the guests assembled for luncheon. They drifted toward the dining room as Mimi was setting the food out on the sideboard. It was a light meal of fancifully cut fruits, a huge salad, cold herbed chicken and hot cornbread with dollops of

butter. As soon as Julian West was settled at the
head of the table, Robert made the announcement
of the invitation. Julian West frowned for a moment, but the rest of the group greeted the information with such enthusiasm that he agreed to go,
albeit with a sense of vague grievance—perhaps
because it was his way, or maybe because the
whole group was going.

Robert said, "I'll go call and accept then."

Lily said, "I want to eavesdrop."

They excused themselves from the table, but as
they approached the telephone in the front entry
hall, Mimi caught their attention. "What's wrong,
Mimi?" Lily asked.

"Well, miss, Professor Hoornart is having a real
hissy fit about some kind of papers he can't find
and wanted to search every room in the house and
that's when I realized that Mrs. Ethridge wasn't at
breakfast and she hasn't come to lunch either. I
kept an eye out for her so I could nip in and tidy
her room while she was out and about and she
hasn't been."

"She's not in the dining room?" Lily said. "No,
I guess not. There were two empty chairs."

"She might be sick, miss."

"Have you knocked on her door?"

"A couple times, miss."

"I'll go see what's become of her," Lily said.

Robert, who had been ringing up the operator,
hung up the phone. "I think it would be better for
me to check on her."

"But Robert . . ." Lily saw his serious expression
and paused. "Very well. But I'll come with you."

They went up to the second floor and Robert
tapped lightly on the door. "Mrs. Ethridge? Are

you all right?" When there was no response, he tapped more firmly and repeated himself loudly.

They stood there, brother and sister, remembering another incident last fall, and staring at each other. "I'll look. You stay out here," Robert said.

He opened the door and almost immediately closed it in Lily's face. She heard the snick of the inside lock. There was complete silence for a long moment, then Robert unlocked and reopened the door. "Lily, she's dead."

Lily gasped. "Are you sure?"

"Quite sure."

"Oh, why did she have to die *here*?" Lily said, then caught herself. "What a selfish thing to say. I'm sorry."

"No need to be. I thought the same thing. It's not as if she's a good friend, or even someone we willingly invited."

"What do we do now?"

"You go back to the dining room and act like nothing's wrong while I call the police and the coroner."

"The police? Why the police?"

"I think you have to call them for an unexplained death. Besides, if we don't, what do we *do* with her? Somebody has to take her away to be buried."

Before she went back to the guests, Lily sneaked into the kitchen where Mrs. Prinney and Mimi were getting the final touches on the dessert. Bud Carpenter was there, too, carefully putting the dessert plates on two large silver trays. Lily told them the bad news.

"Oh, the poor lady," Mimi said. "Was it a heart attack?"

"We don't know for sure," Lily said. "But Robert

is calling Dr. Polhemus and the police. Mimi, could you wait outside for them and try to get them upstairs as quietly and unobtrusively as possible? I'll help carry in the desserts, Mr. Carpenter." She'd forgotten what West had said Bud's rank was.

By the time Lily and Bud got to the dining room, everyone had finished eating and Cecil was questioning them, rather annoyingly, about his missing manuscript and the call he was expecting from his secretary. He didn't actually accuse anyone of taking the manuscript, but he felt sure someone had failed to let him know about his telephone call.

The others were making halfhearted suggestions for places to look for it and Lily suggested that Bud could help Cecil search, if that was all right.

As she spoke, Lily could hear a far-off siren and knew it was coming to Grace and Favor. Why did the new police chief have to turn on the damned noisy thing!

They'd all know in a moment anyway. She might as well tell them before a fleet of cars arrived.

"I'm afraid I have bad news," she said, setting down the tray of powdered sugar–covered pastries in the center of the table. "Mrs. Ethridge has died."

A gasp went around the table. "Oh, no!" Raymond said. "Was it her heart?"

Again, Lily said she didn't know. "The coroner is on his way. So is the police chief. I suppose he has to see to any unexpected death. There's nothing to worry about, but I'd suggest we all stay in here for a while and let Robert take care of things. The police chief might want to ask us questions. And perhaps, Cecil, you could delay your search for just a little while. Until . . ." She was about to say, "Until the body is taken away," but altered it to, "Until everything's taken care of."

"She wasn't old enough to die of heart troubles, was she?" Rachel said, looking stunned.

"Anybody can die of a bad heart," Raymond said. "A friend of mine's father died at thirty-five from a bad heart." He got up from the table and took Lily's hand. "I'm so sorry this has happened. You must realize than none of consider it your fault in any way. These things happen. It's a pity it happened when you had guests."

Lily nearly melted at his firm grasp of her hand and his understanding. She had to hold back her tears. "Still, it's very awkward," she sniffled.

"Not at all," Raymond assured her. "Now sit down and relax. We'll just let the authorities do whatever needs to be done."

Lily had found Raymond a virtual stranger until now. The suave, handsome and sophisticated man-about-town he'd become had erased her memory of what a nice, considerate young man he'd been when they'd both been at school. Now she remembered. And was grateful.

The police chief and coroner arrived with a couple of deputies and crashed around in the entry hall. The table of guests fell silent. Lily caught another familiar voice as well. Jack Summer. The editor of the *Voorburg-on-Hudson Times*. How did he know so quickly? Probably his deputy sheriff second cousin Ralph told him there had been a death at Grace and Favor. He'd done that once before, the busybody!

They could faintly hear footsteps and muffled conversations in the hall above. It was only a quarter of an hour later when the police chief arrived in the dining room, though it seemed like hours.

"Good afternoon," he said, "I'm Chief Howard Walker. I have a few questions to ask of you. I wonder if Miss Brewster would come along first and find a room for us to use."

Mr. Prinney, who had been as silent as the grave and watching Lily carefully, said, "You can use my office on the other side of the entry hall. I'll show you where it is."

He ushered Howard Walker and Lily to the small office and snagged Robert along the way. Robert had been standing at the foot of the stairs, glancing periodically up the stairs.

Mr. Prinney unlocked his office door, showed them all into the room and took a seat at his desk.

Chief Walker sat in a chair with his back to the window so he could see everyone in a good light. "Mr. Prinney, I prefer to talk to people in the house individually," Walker said.

"I know you must want to, but I can't allow it in this case. I'm the Brewsters' attorney and the executor of the estate. I'm afraid I have to stay and hear what you ask."

Walker, a young man who looked vaguely American Indian, had been the town council's choice of replacement for the former police chief, a slovenly, stupid man. Walker was the opposite in every way. He was well dressed in a blue suit, crisp white shirt and red tie. He knew as well as anyone that his most fervent supporter in the town council's choice of him as chief of police was Mr. Prinney.

"I suppose it won't hurt. But I do need to know about this woman who died here." He took out a small black notebook from an inside jacket pocket, rummaged for a pencil and opened the notebook.

"We have no secrets," Mr. Prinney said.

"Very good. Was she a friend of the family or relative?"

"No," Lily said. "I had met her once as a child. She heard that we were having Julian West, the writer, as a guest with the others and invited herself."

"So you know very little about her?" Walker asked.

"Not very much at all. I kept her note somewhere. I can give you her address so you can notify someone at her home. I believe she has a brother in the City. The brother's driver brought her in a car of his."

"When did she retire to her room last night?"

Lily thought back. "I walked upstairs with her at about ten-fifteen. My room is closer to the stairs, so I didn't actually see her go to her room, but I assume she did."

"And you didn't think to check on her until an hour ago?" Walker said disbelievingly.

"She didn't come to breakfast, but we didn't know her habits," Lily said, trying not to be defensive. "Lots of people don't like breakfast. Two of the guests went for a walk through the woods with me this morning. Mr. West and his valet went to their rooms, I believe, and my brother took the others to town. It wasn't until lunchtime that she was missed."

"And who discovered that?"

"Our housekeeper, Mimi Smith, brought it to my attention."

Robert said, "As soon as we realized no one had

seen her all morning, we went to her room. I found her dead."

"The room was unlocked?"

"Nearly everything here is unlocked except this office, the pantry, Mr. Prinney's safe, the wine cellar and the bookcases—for some unknown reason. Before we had guests here, we installed simple latch locks on the inside of the guest room doors. But her door wasn't locked when Lily and I went to her room. We did tell everyone that there was a safe in the house where any valuables they were worried about could be put."

"And the latch lock showed no sign of forcing," Walker asked.

"I didn't notice," Robert replied.

"Was she friendly with anyone here?" Walker asked.

"Not to say friendly," Lily said. And deciding that honesty was the best policy, she added, after a heavy sigh, "Mrs. Ethridge claimed that another of our invited guests, Miss Addie Jonson, had urged her to come. But Addie denies it and I believe her."

"That must have been awkward," Walker said with a glance that could only be called hooded.

"You'll have to ask Miss Jonson about that," Lily said. "It wasn't awkward for us until we found out she was here under false pretenses. Except for Mr. West and his valet, these are all paying guests, Chief Walker. We needed another to make money on the venture and were originally glad Mrs. Ethridge wanted to come."

"You need to make money on guests?" Walker replied with surprise.

"Are you suggesting that's illegal?" Mr. Prinney

put in quickly. "Mr. and Miss Brewster are not idle sloths on the fabric of society," he said and paused, wondering why he'd made such a mixed metaphor. "Why should they not wish to make their home available to paying guests?"

That took Walker down a notch. "It isn't illegal. It's just odd. And it's the odd facts that often unravel a crime."

"Has there, in fact, been a crime?" Mr. Prinney asked.

"Oh, yes. Your unwelcome guest was strangled quite efficiently," Howard Walker said.

Chapter 12

"She was murdered?" Lily asked weakly. "Are you sure?"

"Quite sure," Howard Walker said.

"But who—?"

"That's the important question, isn't it? You said one of your guests knew her. Did any of the others?"

"Mrs. Ethridge claimed to have known Julian West when they were young, although I couldn't be sure he remembered her," Lily said. "And Raymond and Rachel Cameron talked to her a bit about mutual friends, but I didn't have the impression that they'd ever met her."

"What was your feeling about her?"

"I have to admit I didn't much like her," Lily said. "She'd apparently lied about Addie asking her to come. And she was a . . ." Lily paused, trying to find the right word. "She was a manipulator. In the very sweetest way."

"Explain that, please," Walker said.

"Just little things. She arrived too early and she knew it, but claimed to have a good excuse. She had to rest, she needed to eat 'just a little something' and had to have it brought to her room even though our staff was all obviously busy getting ready for the rest of the guests. She asked for a tiny dab of caviar with her snack. It was all very polite and helpless and feminine, but she seemed to me to be quite accustomed to charming people into doing exactly what she wanted. I may be being unfair to her, and might have liked her if I'd gotten to know her better."

Walker shook his head. "First impressions are often the most accurate. What was her relationship to your friend Miss Jonson?"

"It's not my business to talk about that," Lily said firmly. "I heard two entirely different versions of their relationship and I believe Addie's. You need to question her about it. She'll be ruthlessly honest. She always is."

"Was the other version Mrs. Ethridge's?"

"It was, but I won't repeat it until you've talked to Addie."

"Very well. Would you be willing to stay while I question Miss Jonson?"

"Only if it's all right with Addie," Lily said. And then she suddenly remembered that Robert had been calling the Roosevelt home when the whole horror had started.

"Chief Walker, we've been invited to the Governor's house tomorrow. We need to respond to the invitation. May we go?"

At this, he showed surprise again. "You're friends with Governor Roosevelt?"

"No, but he found out that we were hosting Mr. West, and Mrs. Roosevelt very kindly invited Julian West and the rest of us to tea tomorrow."

Walker thought for a moment. "Somebody is a

murderer. It's most likely one of your guests or someone who lives here. Certainly you don't think it's wise to drag that person, whoever it is, to the Governor's house?"

He had a point, but Lily didn't like the inclusion of the household residents among the suspects. "Perhaps you and a deputy could come along."

"Perhaps," he said with a slight smile. "Let's leave this for another hour. I'll let you know then."

Did he think he would solve the murder within a mere hour? Lily wondered.

"May I go back to our guests?" Robert asked.

"In a moment. I have a few questions for you. You're quite certain you didn't use a key to open the door to the victim's room?"

"I am. The only way to lock the room was with a latch inside. When we came to live here, most of the keys to everything had gone missing."

"Did you touch anything in the room?"

"Good Lord, no!" Robert said, offended. "Why would I? I saw that her lips were blue, that she wasn't breathing, and I touched only her hand briefly, which was quite cold. I thought that it was reasonable to assume she was dead, or as near to it as a person can be."

"Did you take her pulse?"

"I wouldn't know how," Robert admitted.

"How long were you in the room?" Walker asked, taking notes on what Robert was saying.

Robert glanced at Lily. "Maybe thirty seconds? Or less?"

"I agree," Lily said.

"Did you know Mrs. Ethridge before she arrived here, Mr. Brewster?"

"Never laid eyes on the woman or even heard of

her until my sister showed me her letter wishing
to be invited," Robert answered curtly.

"Then you may go," Walker said.

"What am I to tell the rest of the guests?"

"You're welcome to tell them she was murdered
and that none of them is free to leave."

"Oh, they'll be happy to hear that!" Robert
snapped.

Walker ignored this show of bad temper.
"Would you ask Miss Jonson to come in?"

Mr. Prinney, content that he had protected the
Brewsters' interests, rose from his desk and left the
room. "I'll look for her, if you wish," he said.

"Don't bother, Mr. Prinney, I'll get her," Lily
said. She wanted a word with Robert. As she and
Mr. Prinney left the room and caught up to Robert,
she whispered to the two of them, "What do we
do about that invitation? We can't show up at the
Governor's house under armed guard."

Mr. Prinney said, "Walker's not going to let us
go. He'd like to go himself—you saw that hint of
smile—but he can't risk it. He might allow West to
go and accompany him, but how could he explain
how their guest needs an escort who happens to be
a police officer?"

"And how do we explain why we can't come?"

"Easy. Blame it on West," Robert said.

"But it isn't *his* fault."

"We don't really know that, do we, Lily?"

Mr. Prinney cleared his throat disapprovingly.

Addie was truthful. "I hated that woman," she announced to Chief Howard Walker. "But I didn't kill
her. Robert said she was murdered." She glanced
at Lily instead of Walker for confirmation.

"Why did you hate her?" Walker asked.

"She seduced away a man I loved a great deal and planned to marry," Addie said bluntly. But there were no tears this time. "He was in poor health and she left him alone to die."

"But you didn't kill her," Walker said.

"I had reason to. I did not do so. But I don't mind a bit that someone did kill her, if that's your next question."

If she expected Walker to show any shock at this remark, she was disappointed.

He only asked, "Who do you think did kill her?"

Addie shrugged. "I have no idea. But you might ask Julian West about her. She was claiming to Lily that she and Julian were 'acquaintances' in their youth. That's not the version she told me."

"Tell me that one," Walker said, licking the point of his pencil.

"Before I knew Anthony—he was the man I was to marry—I knew Lorna. She'd served on the board of the school where I taught. For some reason she decided to be chummy with me. I must have looked like a gullible listener. She told me about her relationship with Julian West."

Addie went on to recount what she could remember of Lorna's story. Lorna had been, she said, a part-time worker at the library where he did a lot of his research in Washington, D.C. He often asked her for help in finding government documents for his research. They started seeing each other. First lunches at a nearby park, then he'd have his driver take them around sightseeing, and eventually it was evenings with just the two of them at the small apartment he kept in Washington.

"She was a bit smirky about that, as if I couldn't be expected to understand about sex. They were to be married, but he went to the Great War and left her a letter. He said he and his cousin and their manservant might not ever come back and that she must forget him as he had a strong premonition that he would die."

"Did you think this story was true?" Walker asked.

"I guess I did at the time," Addie said. "She gave lots of little details that made it seem true and I believed it. But as I came to know her better, I stopped believing anything she said. She might have just made it all up to impress or shock me. Though I can't imagine why she'd enjoy doing that."

"What kind of details?" Lily asked.

Addie crossed her legs and sat back. "Oh, things like how he was so private and wouldn't take her to his home upstate. That she asked about his cousin John and he would say 'He's my cousin, what is there to know?' And when she asked about his manservant—I assume that's the man he brought with him here—he wouldn't talk about him either."

Addie lowered her voice. "She liked knowing things about people. She told me, and I don't know if this is true either, that she didn't ever contact West again. That he was so charming and handsome and intelligent, but also so secretive and reclusive that she didn't feel he'd make a good husband after all. She'd turned it around that she rejected him, rather than being rejected."

Walker tapped his pencil on his knee. "I guess I'll have to ask him about this. Was there any sort of passionate greeting when they met here? I mean passion in all its senses. Joy or hatred."

Lily answered. "Remarkably little. I wouldn't have guessed they had such a history and this is the first I've heard of it. Bud Carpenter just said something like, 'Oh, Captain West, it's Miss Lorna Pratt,' and West greeted her politely. There was no particular sign of like or dislike on either side."

"That was my feeling as well," Addie said. "Ships that had passed in the night," she said, then blushing slightly added, "So to speak."

"Did either of you suspect she'd come here to renew their 'friendship'?"

That was a tactful way to put it, Lily thought.

"She only told me she admired his books and had known him when they were young," Lily said. "There was no hint of any strong ties or lingering resentment or anything else."

Walker continued to tap his pencil on his knee. "Miss Jonson, were you in your own room all night?"

"Yes. And," she added, determined to let him know the worst. "my room is connected by a bathroom, closet and small hallway to Lorna's room."

"Did you lock your outside hall door and the one that connected with hers?"

"I did. I didn't want to have any intimate chats with her."

"Had she locked her side?" Walker asked.

Addie looked surprised and offended. "I wasn't interested in finding out. I have no idea."

"Did you hear anything overnight? Any conversation from her room?"

"I wouldn't have with the passage between the rooms and both doors closed."

"No hint of any unusual sounds overnight?" Walker persisted.

"I sleep like a fallen log, sir. Always have. I heard nothing."

When Addie was excused, Walker asked Lily to stay behind. "What she said about the man she intended to marry—was that what she told you?"

"Yes, but in more detail."

"And Mrs. Ethridge told you another version, I believe you said?" Walker had taken over Mr. Prinney's chair, presumably as the more authoritative position.

"She claimed that Addie had forced herself on Mr. Ethridge. That he had no real interests in common with her, as he had with Lorna. That he'd broken off the engagement with Addie of his own accord, with advice from Lorna, with whom he was seriously, and mutually, in love. That was the gist of it, anyway."

"Is that story believable from what you know of your friend Miss Jonson?"

Lily hated being asked this. "It could be," she said reluctantly. "She gets enormous enthusiasms and pursues them avidly."

"And you hadn't heard the story before about Mrs. Ethridge's relationship with Julian West?"

"Addie doesn't gossip about anybody. She only told me about her own troubles with Lorna Ethridge because we're good friends," Lily said and started to leave the room. She turned and asked, "Have you had lunch? We probably have a lot of food left over. I could bring you a plate."

"Just bring me your famous guest," Walker said. "I presume you have a room I can have. I'm not leaving here until I know who killed this woman."

"Yes, plenty of rooms," Lily said, turning to leave.

"And call the Governor's home and tell them that you won't be coming to visit tomorrow," Walker added.

Chapter 13

Julian West had gone back to his room. Lily had, against all common sense, looked for him all over the ground floor and outside first, reluctant to beard the Great Man in his temporary den. Eventually she gave up and knocked at his door, which Bud Carpenter opened.

"Yes, Miss Brewster?"

"I need to speak to Mr. West."

"The Captain's quite busy," Carpenter said, starting to close the door.

Lily slipped her foot in the way. "I'm sure he is, but the police chief wishes to speak to him. And I'm afraid everyone must stay here and we're canceling the meeting with Governor Roosevelt."

"How very disappointing," Bud said blandly.

"It is, indeed." She stepped into the room. Suitcases were open on the bed and obviously being packed. Julian West had his shaving kit in hand and had just come from the hall to the bath and large dressing room Bud occupied.

Lily gave her messages again. A little more briskly this time.

"Why should the police chief have any interest in me?" West demanded.

"He's interviewing everyone," Lily said and turned away.

"Well, he's not keeping me here," West said.

"We'll see about that," Lily muttered to herself as she went back to the library. It was where she always went when she needed comfort and calm. She stood on the small balcony where she could see the river below. *Damn Lorna Pratt Ethridge for getting herself killed at Grace and Favor*, she thought unreasonably.

She heard the door to the library open and assumed it was Robert, which it was. And he had Jack Summer with him. Jack was the editor of the *Voorburg-on-Hudson Times* and one of the first people Lily and Robert had met when they arrived in Voorburg. He was about their own ages, midtwenties, short and with a remarkable resemblance to James Cagney. He had the same crinkly hair, bantam rooster strut, swagger and energy of a tightly coiled spring. And with his recently increased salary he must have been attending the talkies in town and had decided to imitate the young star's curt style. Lily hoped it was only a passing fancy.

"What's going on here?" he said. "Howard Walker won't tell me a thing."

"How did you know anything was going on?" Lily asked. "Your blabby cousin?"

"Ralph keeps me up on local events," Jack said. "So who died? And how?"

"A guest. And she was murdered, Chief Walker says," Robert answered.

"You still having your dinner tonight?" Jack

asked, without sounding the least shocked. "You said I could come and interview Julian West."

Lily was on the verge of chiding him for his selfish attitude, but she had her own selfish attitude going on that was equally indefensible.

"Nobody's allowed to leave," she said. "Dinner will be as planned. You're still invited. Though I'm not sure Julian West will be willing to be interviewed after being grilled by Howard Walker."

"Sure he will. Celebrities love to talk about themselves," Jack said without any previous experience with celebrities to back his claim. "So it was a dame that got killed," Jack said, sprawling rudely in one of the massive chairs beside the French windows. "How'd she get done in?" Jack had gone to college and considered proper grammar nearly a God in his newspaper writing, but with his new status as editor, his spoken vocabulary had grown coarser.

"Strangled, we hear," Robert said.

"Name?" Jack asked, getting out his notebook.

"Lorna Pratt Ethridge," Lily said. "I wish I'd never heard of her."

"Putting a crimp in your party, isn't she?" Jack said. "Age of victim?"

"I have no idea. Early to mid-fifties, I'd guess."

"Where's she from? How did you know her? What was she doing here?" He snapped out the questions, tapping his foot impatiently on the floor.

"She's from New York City, now. Or maybe just keeps an apartment there. It was the address she gave. But she also lives in the same town Addie does."

"Addie?"

"A friend of mine who is also here. We didn't know Mrs. Ethridge and we don't really know what she was doing here," Lily said wearily. "She invited herself."

"Who are the other guests? Besides Julian West."

"Do you really need to know all this?" Robert asked.

"Listen, I work for you guys. You own the paper. Want me to do my job or not?"

This wasn't strictly true, but nobody had ever told Jack that Lily and Robert wouldn't really own anything for another nine years and six months and only then if they stayed in Voorburg virtually the whole time. Meanwhile, the entire estate they'd inherited was in the hands of Mr. Prinney, the estate's executor. It had apparently never occurred to Jack to check out their uncle's will at the county courthouse, for which they were glad.

"Miss Addie Jonson, my friend and former teacher," Lily said. "Mr. West and his manservant, Sergeant Bud Carpenter. Professor Cecil Hoornart, the biographer and book reviewer. If you haven't heard of him, you'd do well to pretend to have. I think he's a bit prickly about his intellectual achievements. Raymond and Rachel Cameron. They're school friends of ours."

"That's all?"

Robert said, "You forgot Mad Henry."

"I'm *trying* to forget Mad Henry," Lily said. "Where is he, anyway?"

"Probably in the basement, tinkering with his system."

"Mad Henry?" Jack asked. "He sounds like a good suspect."

"Henry Trover is a friend of Robert's," Lily said. "And he's only mad in harmless ways. He's an inventor. Of pretty useless things."

"So what's your best guess?"

"Guess?" Robert asked.

"Who bumped the old girl off?"

"Good Lord! How would *we* know?" Lily exclaimed.

"You're the 'lord and lady' of the manor," Jack said. "Surely you have some idea what's going on in your own mansion."

"You'd think so," Robert said. "But you're wrong. And if we did suspect someone, we wouldn't say so. And you wouldn't put it in the paper if you had someone in mind."

"Guess I'll have to corner Howard Walker," Jack said, unoffended by this edict.

"Good luck," Lily said. "He isn't as gabby, or as stupid, as the old police chief. Nor such a bully."

"Naw. He's an okey-doke guy, our Walker. You know he's part Indian, don't you? When the Munsee tribe of the Delawares got run out of the valley about a hundred years ago, a few who had intermarried with the Dutch got left behind. He's the great-great-grandson of one of them. Or maybe three 'greats.'"

"How do you happen to know this?" Robert asked.

"I'm planning to do a piece in the paper about him. I was going to run it this week, but I think your murder is going to take precedence."

"It's not *our* murder," Lily said.

Jack shrugged this off. "You don't mind if I question some of your guests, do you?"

"We certainly do mind," Robert said. "It's bad enough that this happened. We don't want them harassed by a reporter."

"Editor *and* reporter," Jack said.

* * *

Addie had gone to lie down in her room. She locked the door between the bath and closet to Lorna's room. They'd taken Lorna's body away, but she could still smell Lorna's perfume lingering. Or she imagined she could. Or maybe it was the sick, sweet odor of death. Like a rose on the verge of rot.

Addie knew she was the prime suspect. And she also knew that nothing she could say would make a difference if this Walker person was stupid enough to go on instinct instead of proof. After all, she had the motive. Nobody else did.

Unless by some freak chance Lorna had told part of the truth about her youthful relationship with Julian West and there had been more to the story. But what motive could West have? He'd thrown Lorna over fifteen years or so earlier. They'd gone their own ways.

"I was hurt at first," Lorna had told her years ago when Addie thought they were friends before Anthony came along. "Any girl would have been. But after a while I realized that I would have broken it off sooner or later anyway. Marriage had to be two minds becoming one and Julian wasn't willing for that to happen."

Addie didn't agree in the first place that two minds should be one. And she knew better now than to give any credence to what Lorna said. Had it all been a lie? Had Lorna merely made it up? West had to be prodded into remembering who she was. But Carpenter had tipped him off the moment they entered the yellow parlor. But maybe that was just Carpenter's way. To get the first word in and act the "perfect servant." But West hadn't seemed especially pleased or displeased to greet Lorna. There was nothing but mere courtesy in his greeting to her.

An unlikely casting for "first assassin."

Addie also qualified as prime suspect because she had the greatest access to Lorna. It would have been easy to just tiptoe through the little hallway with the bath on one side and the closet on the other. She alone of the whole house party wouldn't have needed to risk being seen in the hall. She could have slipped right through the hall, choked the life out of the despicable woman and gone back to bed. In theory. Surely Walker was considering this.

As she started feeling worn and tired, Addie closed her eyes. What about the rest of them? Had others had relationships with Lorna that they'd forgotten or pretended to have forgotten? Surely Lorna didn't pick out Addie as her only challenge. Lorna was the type who always had to have what she wanted. She'd taken Anthony from Addie. Had she taken something else half so valuable from someone else at Grace and Favor who resented her even more than Addie did?

Perhaps someone Lorna had forgotten she'd ever known and done an ill-deed. Or someone who had a loved one who suffered at Lorna's pretty, pampered hands. There had to be a logical explanation. Nobody in the whole crowd seemed like a natural-born killer. And even Julian West hadn't suggested that he, his cousin or Bud had actually killed anyone in the Great War. They'd been support staff, not fighters.

But maybe it was someone none of them had met. A person who waited, watched her, followed her here and sneaked into the house to kill her and let the others, Addie in particular, become the suspects. Was Chief Howard Walker bright enough or experienced enough to think of that?

Raymond Cameron was pacing around the front of the house under the watchful eye of a deputy. "Can't leave the house, sir," the deputy said.

"I'm not leaving," Raymond said. "We were told we couldn't. I just had to get some fresh air."

"Just stay in sight, then," the deputy said. "Five minutes is all."

Raymond went over and sat on a bench that had been built around a shady tree. An oak, he guessed. And the bench was new, still oozing a little sap through the clean white paint. He spread out his monogrammed handkerchief to sit on so he wouldn't ruin his trousers. He leaned back against the tree, half turned away from the deputy.

Let him just stand there like a lump and stare at me, he thought. *You don't recognize me any more than Lorna did.*

She'd looked straight through him. If he'd known she was going to be here, he wouldn't have come. He wouldn't have even replied to Lily's invitation. The minute he saw her, however, floods of memory engulfed him.

That summer when he was eighteen he had worked in his uncle's office, to see if he had taste for the legal profession and would wish to pursue it when he entered college in the fall, only to find that Uncle Joseph just wanted an errand boy, not someone to mentor. His parents wouldn't allow him to quit the job and go to Europe for the rest of

the summer as he wanted to do. Until he met
Lorna.

He'd been so damned innocent. She must have
been nearly as old as his mother, but nothing like
a mother. More like a slightly aging goddess to his
then-naive eyes. A small woman, with generous,
soft-looking breasts, a small waist and such grace.

He never learned what business she had with his
Uncle Joseph. Just that it involved a fair amount of
paperwork that had to be carted around and
signed. Probably some elaborate property
exchange, since that's what Uncle Joe usually dealt
with. The first time she came into the office, she
had something to sign and date that required a witness to the signature. Raymond was called into the
office.

"This is Mrs. Ethridge, a widow known to me,
Raymond," Uncle Joseph said, "but as her repre-
sentative, I shouldn't be the signing witness. Will
you watch her sign and then sign below with your
name and your parents' address?"

Raymond's hand had almost trembled in her
presence. The smell of her perfume, something like
roses on a warm day, made his senses reel.

"Get Mrs. Ethridge a cab when we're through,
Raymond," Uncle Joe said. "And you might as well
go on home. We're about through for the day."

Mrs. Ethridge ("Oh, Raymond, you must call me
Lorna") took his arm as they entered the elevator.
He imagined he could feel the warmth of her body
next to his. Outside, she still clung to him as he
hailed a cab and when he handed her inside, she
leaned forward and gestured to him to come along
with her. She gave the address of the hotel she was
staying in and let him pay for the cab, but with

that small hand still draped over his arm. He followed her to her room.

She invited him into the rather luxurious suite, lifted her light veil and removed her hat. And then her hairpins. And then her shoes.

"Raymond, you're going to be a fine young man someday, but I can tell that there's a lot you need to know."

For three days, when he was supposed to be bringing her documents ("I don't mind that you take the time to be polite to her, Raymond, she's a good client," Uncle Joe had said), she was his sexual mentor. He fancied himself in love with her and she with him, but when the three days were over, and she disappeared without a word of farewell, he realized it had been otherwise.

He'd been an experiment. A raw, awkward young man, irresistibly drawn to a very experienced woman who saw him as an essay on clumsiness and modesty that, for some reason, she needed to revise.

What on earth had that reason been? He'd never been able to guess. Was it revenge on some other man? An emotional upset that required an impersonal outlet? Had she just had a fright, or a close call with death or illness and needed to know she could wrap some young healthy male around her little finger?

After he recovered from his initial shock at her disappearance, he tried to figure her out. He tried to convince himself that she *had* in fact loved him, but something 'bigger than both of them' had made her retreat. But knew it wasn't true.

Was she a benefactor? Yes, in many ways. He'd gone from child to man in that week. A long over-

due and somehow frightening change. Had she
loved him? Clearly not. After the first day she'd
never called him by name again. As if she'd forgotten what it was and felt awkward asking. After
another two months of puzzling over the experience, he settled into a quiet resentment of the
woman. He kept remembering things she'd said
that didn't sound offensive at the time, but now
annoyed him.

"Get rid of those glasses. You don't need them
and they make you look stupid, not smart like you
imagine."

"Grow your hair a bit longer. Don't keep hanging on to your childhood."

"Don't grab a woman's breast as if you're milk-
ing a cow."

"Sir, your five minutes are up," the deputy called
out.

"They are not," Raymond said curtly without
even turning around.

He was still in a state of shock that the goddess
or devil, whichever she had been, had been introduced to him at Grace and Favor, had shaken his
hand in a calm and courteous manner, and had
dismissed him with a glance.

And then someone had murdered her.

Chapter 14

Howard Walker continued to work his way through the guests and household, asking a lot of questions, raising some hackles. When he finally managed to get Julian West into Mr. Prinney's office, there was some unintelligible shouting from the Great Man, who exited the office brusquely and stomped back up to his room.

Bud Carpenter, ramrod stiff and giving the impression he was wearing a uniform, although he wasn't, was next. Robert hung around the entryway, trying to eavesdrop while pretending to look for missing car keys, which only Lily knew Robert would never lose.

"Couldn't decipher a word," Robert reported to her.

Raymond Cameron spent a very short time being interviewed and came out of the office looking utterly unconcerned. The same was true of Rachel.

Cecil Hoornart looked worried when he was called in.

"Professor Hoornart, I hear you're missing something," Walker said.

"I am. I'm sure now that my paperwork was stolen. I've been retracing every single step I took since I last saw the work."

"And what is it that's missing?"

"Three years' worth of research and writing on my biography of Julian West."

"Was Mrs. Ethridge mentioned anywhere?"

"No. The first I ever heard of her was when I arrived at Grace and Favor."

"Do you think the possible theft of this research has anything to do with her death?"

Howard Walker had been a deputy for three years before he decided he wanted to study law. He'd attended a small law school upstate for barely a year when the financial crisis interfered with his education. But he knew from experience how important academic research was and how jealously a professional guarded it. And as Cecil Hoornart was a professional academic, he trusted his views.

Cecil was surprised at the question. "I can't imagine how." He thought for a long moment. "No, I don't think so. Do you?"

Howard Walker wasn't used to being questioned. "Perhaps. Had you learned anything about Julian West that was scandalous in any way?"

Cecil laughed. "You must read the more 'popular' biographies. Unfortunately, I haven't. Though I think most people would be somewhat surprised that he studied for the ministry, as he mentioned last night. There is no suggestion of lingering spirituality in his books. Particularly in the latter ones, which are frankly a bit too far on the grim side for most people, though I respect the work."

"So you know nothing about him that he'd wish to have suppressed?"

"Do you consider him your primary suspect?"
Cecil answered.

"No, merely the most central. That is, he's the
one everybody came here to see and talk with."

Cecil nodded. "Yes, I see that. Everybody here is
a fan of his to some extent. He was the central figure of the gathering. But does that mean anything?"

"That's what I need to find out. And I'm troubled
by your work disappearing. I'll have my deputy
search the house and grounds. You're certain you
didn't lose it yourself?"

"Quite certain. I had it with me last evening
when I interviewed him."

"You interviewed him?"

"He agreed to give me information for the appendix—a list of dates, really. Where and when he
was born, where he was educated, places he'd
lived, his rank and dates of service in the army,
publication dates of his books," Cecil said. "Nothing very interesting or new to me except for the
study for the ministry."

"Could you re-create that information for me?"

"I'm not sure. But I suppose if he told it to me
once, he would tell me again."

"Perhaps later. I just need the basics. I've not
read his books, which puts me at a disadvantage.
I'll have my deputy search if you wouldn't mind
trying to jot down what you can remember."

Cecil went to his room and Walker summoned
Ralph. "Professor Hoornart is missing a manuscript
and some notes of an interview. I think it may be
relevant. Search first anywhere that paper may
have been burned. If you don't find anything, start

looking in cabinets, drawers, under furniture—you know the drill, I hope."

Ralph was thrilled to get to participate in the investigation instead of merely guarding the door. "Yessir!"

"Are they going to be able to leave on Sunday?" Robert asked Lily.

"I hope so," Lily said. She was thinking about money, as usual. If they had to feed all these people for an extra day or two, it would wipe out their meager profit.

When Cecil had returned to his room, Robert took Lily aside in the ballroom, which was unoccupied and so large that they could be sure not to be overheard. "Hoornart's researching West, isn't he? For a biography?" Robert asked his sister.

"Yes."

"Does this mean Walker is focusing on West being the perpetrator?"

"I have no idea," Lily said. "I'd guess from the yelling that West simply refused to give any information about himself and Walker is trying to find out more about him from Cecil Hoornart."

"How much can he know? He's a critic of books, not an acquaintance of West's. I got the impression last night that they'd never met."

Lily thought for a moment. "As Hoornart told me, he's researched basic things about his life. Where and when he was born, what regiment he served in, where he's lived. That sort of thing."

"How would knowing that help Walker's investigation?"

Lily shrugged. "I guess he's just getting background on everyone and West obviously wasn't cooperative. I wish I'd known what he was yelling about. I only caught one phrase about a small town police chief having no business grilling him."

"The man sure knows how to make himself suspicious."

"I'd guess Bud Carpenter smoothed it over. That seems to be his aim in life. To make life easier for West."

"That's exactly the sort of wife I'd like to have someday," Robert said with a grin. "Somebody who would make excuses for my naughty behavior and fetch and carry for me."

"That kind of wife would eventually bore you senseless," Lily said. "You don't think someone like Rachel Cameron would fill that role, do you?"

"Why her in particular?" Robert said warily.

"Because you nearly drool every time you talk to her."

"I do not. But she is a sight for sore eyes."

"I thought you went for brains and beauty. I haven't heard her say much of anything that seems terribly intellectual."

Robert thought for a moment. "I guess you're right. Don't worry that I'll be smitten with her. But she is ornamental. Besides . . . I wouldn't want to be Raymond Cameron's brother-in-law."

"Why not?"

"He's a cold fish."

"He's been very nice to me. Very considerate and sympathetic."

"Now who's sounding gooey?"

"I'm not. I just mean he's a pleasant guest. And I know he's very intelligent. At least he was when I knew him in school and I don't think people get stupider as they age. And he's rather 'ornamental' himself," she said with a smile. "And so is Howard Walker, come to that."

"Are you husband hunting?"

"Good Lord, no! I have enough on my plate with you, this house, my bookkeeping and trying to remember all Mr. Prinney is trying to teach me about the estate. I haven't time for going to the talkies, much less a husband hunt."

She thought for a moment. "Robert, if either of us were to marry, the person would have to live here with us."

"Then we better make damned sure we both like him or her," Robert said. "I've got to get back to looking for my keys."

"The ones that you're jingling in your pocket?"

"Was I? I better stop that. I'll blow my cover."

"I don't think anybody believes it anyway. Mrs. Prinney keeps finding things to do in the entry hall. I saw her moving some ornaments around, and even Mimi is doing a furious job of dusting out there. Bud is standing like a statue by the steps asking everyone if there's anything he can do to help. The place is starting to look like Grand Central Station."

Mad Henry tapped on the door of Mr. Prinney's office and came in on Walker's invitation.

"I haven't put a box in here yet. Would this be a good time?" Henry asked.

"A box? Who are you?"

"Henry Trover. I'm putting in a communication system."

"Please sit down, Mr. Trover. I'm Chief Walker. I'm investigating Mrs. Ethridge's death.

"It's a terrible shame, isn't it? But I really know nothing about it."

"Perhaps not, but I'd like to talk to you anyway. This communication thing of yours . . . can you hear what's being said when the mysterious box is installed in a room?"

"That's the point, yes."

"And you've put these boxes in all the other rooms?"

"Just the bedrooms and the yellow parlor and the dining room."

"And can you actually hear things from them. Did you hear things last night?"

"Oh, yes. Most of them seemed to be working quite well."

"Tell me what you heard," Walker said firmly.

"Lots of voices."

"I meant, what they were saying," Walker said. Was this strange young man too stupid or too bright to get his meaning?

"I didn't pay any attention to what was said. I was concerned with the sound quality."

Walker stood up and leaned across the desk menacingly. "Mr. Trover, think very hard. I want to know what you heard."

Henry wasn't especially frightened of him. He didn't recognize that he was supposed to be. So he closed his eyes for a moment and tried very hard to remember. "I heard a woman humming a song. The music was familiar, but the words blurred."

"What woman?"

"Couldn't tell. It might have been Phoebe's voice. And somebody mentioned an appendix."

"Was that Professor Hoornart? He was questioning Mr. West about dates and so forth of his life for an appendix to his book."

"Could have been. And later I heard a woman say, "Oh, Professor Hoornart, wait a moment. I have a local map if you'd like to borrow it. That might have been Phoebe, too."

"And what else?"

"Nothing else. Except snoring. And shuffling noises as people were getting ready for bed."

Walker questioned him more, but got nothing. Henry claimed he just hadn't paid attention. It was merely a test of his system.

Robert and Lily had been lurking outside the door, but hadn't been able to hear very well. They pounced on Henry when he came out of the room and he obligingly repeated his whole conversation with Chief Walker.

The next thing on Lily's mental list was to find Jack Summer. She found him grilling his cousin Ralph, who had finished looking for evidence of paper being burned in the house (they'd have all smelled it anyway) and was looking around in the woods behind the house for a likely spot to burn things.

"Walker hasn't told me anything, Jack. I'm just the toady," Ralph was saying when Lily located them. "He's not a big blabbermouth like that ass Chief Henderson was."

"Jack, could I have a talk with you," Lily interrupted.

"Sure. Have you learned something?"

"Not a thing. But I want to give you a warning. Don't pry into this death at dinner. And don't try to interview Mr. West, either. Before and after, you can make any arrangements you want. But dinner

is off limits. You're a guest, not an editor or reporter then."

Jack frowned. "Okay, but I'm coming early and
staying late. And I'll be at The Fate tomorrow. Tell
me about these people, would you? I know about
West, of course. I read one of his books once.
Didn't like it much. But tell me more about this
woman who died."

Lily said, "I've already told you everything I
know about her. She claimed to be a friend of my
friend Addie, but she wasn't. She wrote and asked
if she could be invited so as to renew an old friendship with West."

"She lied?"

"About that. And probably about other things as
well. But I don't know what."

"You don't sound as if you liked her much."

"I didn't. She was very attractive for her age, and
too-too charming. I suspect everything she did was
an act of some kind. And don't you dare say so in
the paper!"

"No, I won't. I never met her, but I trust your
opinion. So why is Ralph looking for something
that might have been burned?"

"I presume because Cecil Hoornart's manuscript
and notes are missing. They were for his biography
of Julian West."

"You've had a theft as well as a murder?"

"I didn't think so. I thought Professor Hoornart
had just absentmindedly forgotten where he left it.
But he's driven everyone mad looking for it and
now Walker's got Ralph searching as well. Walker
thinks it's important, I guess."

"Which leads us back to West again. But if this
Hoornart fellow knew something he shouldn't

have, wouldn't he have been the victim instead of Mrs. Ethridge?" Jack said as much to himself as Lily.

"I hadn't thought about it that way," Lily said. "If someone really did steal the papers, that wouldn't wipe the important parts out of Cecil's mind. He may still be in danger. I suppose I should mention that to Walker."

"I'm sure he's capable of working it out himself," Jack said. "And the missing manuscript may not be important at all. Maybe someone just snatched it to get a sort of preview of the book he was preparing. Just out of curiosity."

"But who would do that?"

"Isn't your friend Addie rather a brainy sort who reads all his stuff?"

Lily's temper flared. "Why is everybody suspicious of Addie? She's the most forthright, honest person I know."

"Who else is suspicious of her?" Jack asked. "Maybe you?"

"Of course not!" Lily said, stomping away.

"Of course not," she repeated quietly to herself.

Chapter 15

Lily felt if she didn't get out of the mansion for a while, she'd go mad. She tapped on the door to Mr. Prinney's office. Chief Walker was using the phone, but covered the mouthpiece and called, "Come in." The only phone in the house originally was in the entryway, but Mr. Prinney had put in an extra extension in his office for his own business just recently.

She opened the door and said defiantly, "Would you admit I'm the last person who would try to get away from here?" Lily asked.

He smiled. "I suppose so."

"Then I'm going for a walk." She closed the door and turned to find Raymond standing behind her.

"I'll come with you, if you don't mind," he said.

"Not at all. Let's go out the back way through the kitchen."

There were a few people Lily didn't know on the lawn behind the house. They were setting up card tables for the fête. She smiled and nodded nicely to them, and led Raymond around toward the library windows where the lawn sloped down to the river below. "Do you think they know what happened here?" Lily said, tipping her head toward the handful of townspeople.

"In my limited experience, I think people in small towns probably know everything," Raymond said, taking her arm. "That's probably why they're setting things up today. Surely tomorrow morning would be time enough."

They reached a bench under some trees where a truly majestic view of the river spread out below. It was one of Lily's favorite spots, and in good weather, she often spent an afternoon there reading, napping, brushing out her dog Agatha or just daydreaming while watching the traffic on the river and the trains racing back and forth alongside it on both sides of the water.

"It's nice here," Raymond said. "Nice to be with you, too." He laid his arm along the back of the bench and put his hand on her arm, sketching a slow pattern of strokes.

Lily was surprised and flattered. She'd worried needlessly about having to apologize for her behavior so many years ago. He'd apparently either forgotten or forgiven.

They chatted about the river, admired a fine sailboat skirting its way like a dancer around a line of barges. Raymond gently pulled her closer. She turned to say something and before she could speak, he'd enveloped her in a hug and was teasingly kissing her.

"Raymond, we're in full view of the house," Lily said. It wasn't that she didn't like being kissed. But not in front of any gawker who might be looking out from the library or bedroom windows that faced the river. Especially if it might be Chief Walker. She certainly didn't want to have to explain her whole past to him. And if Robert saw them, he'd rag on her about it forever.

She pulled away and stood up. "I should get back. I'm the hostess of this party and need to be on duty," she said with a smile.

Raymond said nothing, just looked past her at the river. *Was he angry?* Lily wondered. Then asked herself if she really cared if he was as she made her way up the slight slope.

She was just going upstairs to comb her hair and freshen her lipstick when she met Mimi coming down the stairs. Mimi looked upset. "What's wrong, Mimi?"

Mimi shook her head and gestured toward Lily's room. Lily followed and closed the door behind them. "What is it?" she said very quietly.

Mimi had a wad of sheets under her arm. "I was tidying up Mrs. Ethridge's room. The policeman told me I could."

Lily frowned. "I should have done that myself, Mimi. Was it awful?"

"No, miss. Just some stains."

"Oh . . ." Lily said, gulping.

"Not that kind of stains, miss. But I found a couple things. I don't like talking to the police much, so I was looking for you."

She set the sheets down on the floor and unwrapped the corner of the bundle. "This was in the bed," she said, handing Lily a page of perfumed letter paper. Lily recognized it as Lorna's. It was the same as the paper she'd used to contact them in the first place. It had been crumpled. Lily flattened it out and read.

"Raymond dear, it's been a long time, hasn't it? Come to my room tomorrow night, I have something so interesting to tell y—" The writing stopped mid-word.

Lily gasped. "Oh, dear."

"That's not all, Miss Lily," Mimi said, handing her a little gold piece of jewelry. "I don't rightly know what this is."

Lily stared at the tie tack and sighed. "I do. It belongs to Mr. West. He was wearing it on his tie last night. Where did you find it?"

"It was under the bed, miss. Mrs. Ethridge's bed."

For anyone else to have even noticed something so small under a bed would have been remarkable, but Mimi's housekeeping skills knew no bounds. When she cleaned a room, she really cleaned.

"I'll take it to the sheriff. His people certainly didn't do a good job of checking the room."

"No, miss. But the letter was crammed down between the top sheet and the bedspread. And so was a fountain pen. With the cap off. That's what the stains are. It leaked. I don't think I can get the ink out of the sheet. May I have it for rags?"

"Of course. But the police should have checked the whole room instead of making you do their work. Don't mention finding these to anyone else."

Lily put the letter and the tie tack into a pillowcase and went to Mr. Prinney's office.

"Come in," Walker said impatiently. He was on the telephone again. Or still. He glared at Lily for interrupting him.

"I think you better get off the phone and look at something."

Glaring even more fiercely, he brought his conversation to an abrupt end. Lily opened the pillowcase and handed him the contents.

"Good God!" Walker said as he read the note. "Where did you find this?"

"The housekeeper found it in the bedding when she remade the bed. Your people should have searched the room more diligently."

"You're damned right. I thought they knew what to do, but I was wrong. Heads will roll," Walker said. "And the tie tack? Was that in the bed as well?"

"Under it. It's Julian West's. I noticed it last night. His was gold and it has a very tiny diamond in the middle that catches the light. I'm sure it's the same one."

"I suppose you realize that Raymond Cameron told me that he'd never met or heard of this woman before. But she was writing him a very personal note. And Julian West absolutely denies having even remembered Mrs. Ethridge until his man reminded him of her name, and yet he left a tie tack in her room."

Lily shrugged. "Maybe. He could have lost it somewhere else and she picked it up intending to return it to him."

Walker looked embarrassed. "Possible, but not likely. What on earth was the woman doing?"

"Counting coup," Lily said.

At this, Walker suddenly laughed. "I didn't know anyone but Indians knew that phrase. Yes, that's what it looks like. I'm going to have a few searing words with my deputies, if you don't mind excusing me. And then with Raymond Cameron and Julian West."

But Lily caught up with Raymond first. He was coming in the kitchen door as she went to consult with Mrs. Prinney about dinner. "Raymond, could you wait for me a moment?" Lily asked.

She hastily finished her conversation with Mrs. Prinney and led him to the front hall. "Am I mistaken, or was Mrs. Ethridge a stranger to you?"

"Complete stranger. Why?"

"I just wondered."

"We did have some friends in common, as it happens. But I'd never even heard of her before I met her here."

"I see," Lily said. "Chief Walker would like to speak to you in a little bit. After he's finished slaughtering his deputies."

"Lily, what's going on? Why are you being so mysterious," he said, putting his hand on her shoulder. "Kind of funny, his being called Chief Walker. He looks so much like an Indian."

She stepped back, rather than blatantly shaking off his touch. "He is part Indian and I wouldn't try that joke on him if I were you. And I don't really know what's going on, but I intend to find out. I've got to see Robert to check on the drinks for tonight."

Instead, she went to her room first and got a handkerchief and rubbed it violently on her lips to eradicate his kiss of half an hour earlier. How could she have been so dim? There she was, letting him paw at her, when Lorna Ethridge, had she not died, would have slipped her note to him today. A note that clearly indicated that he knew her all too well. She'd been so stupidly enthralled with his apparent sympathy that she forgot that he, too, was a suspect in Lorna's death. And, it appeared, might well have a motive in spite of his lie that he'd never met her.

Lily went looking for Robert to tell him what Mimi had discovered. She found him outside, visiting with a group of townswomen who were setting up a display to show off their quilting. All of them, including the oldest, a great-grandmother, were flirting with him. Much as she hated to ruin their fun, she drew Robert away.

"She was writing a personal note to Raymond?" he exclaimed as they strolled toward the woods. "I told you he was a bad'un. This proves it. Don't ever let yourself be alone with him, Lily."

"I don't really need to be told that, Robert," she said huffily. 'But . . .'"

"But what?"

"Maybe Raymond didn't really know her before he came here. Maybe she was just pretending they were old . . . 'friends.' She lied about other things, why not that too? Maybe Raymond is the one telling the truth." But the words rang hollow.

"Then she wouldn't have addressed him as 'Raymond, dear.' 'Dear Raymond' might make sense. 'Raymond, dear' is much different. They couldn't have gotten on that sort of terms so quickly."

"How would you know that?"

"She was a hot old number," Robert said. "You said she'd told Addie that she and West were lovers and he didn't seem to remember her any more than Raymond did. Whatever else you could say about Mrs. Ethridge, she *wasn't* an unforgettable woman."

"We'll never forget her, for certain," Lily said curtly. After a moment's thought, she asked, "Is there any innocent reason West's tie tack would have been in her room?"

Robert rolled his eyes. "I thought you were too

sophisticated to ask a question like that."

"I'm serious. I don't want to think our guest of honor is a killer. I thought maybe he lost it and she found it and possibly set it on the night table to give back in the morning and it got knocked to the floor by the person who strangled her."

Robert curled his lip. "He just forgot to put it back on when he was getting redressed in her room, Lily."

Lily ignored this. "I know! She could have stolen it from his room. Remember when that girl—what was her name? Bitsy? Betsy? She had a crush on you and stole little mementoes? She took your gold cigarette lighter and a table napkin you'd written something on? And gave them back to you in a huff when she saw you out with someone else? Remember?"

"She was seventeen years old, Lily, and an idiot. Lorna Ethridge was neither. She was, it appears, a full-fledged seducer."

"So why didn't she go after you?" Lily asked.

"She did."

"No!"

"It didn't work," Robert said with a grin. "And I'm not going to share the details. It wasn't a pretty scene."

"That horrible woman! Robert, I'm simply outraged!"

"So was someone else," he said. "And it was probably Julian West."

"Look, Robert, he's not a likable person, but that doesn't mean he's a murderer."

"He was in the war. He writes war novels. He's seen and experienced and written about a lot of horrible deaths. That sort of life is bound to make a person callous about life and death."

"But he wasn't killing people in the war. He was an observer and helping take the dead and injured back. And even if he had, it doesn't mean anything. Lots of men came back from the war and are living perfectly normal lives with no urge to bump people off."

"But they were nice people to begin with. Julian West was at the front lines. He saw his own cousin die. And many, many others as well. And he's a nasty, surly man besides. Probably always was. He could kill someone without turning a hair," Robert said.

Chapter 16

"You're sure I haven't received a telephone call?" Cecil asked Lily.

"I'm sorry, but no. Chief Walker's had the telephone tied up though."

"I'm going to have to call my secretary then. I was expecting to hear from her today and it's almost four now. I'll give you the money for the call."

Lily would have liked to be gracious and decline the offer of money, but she couldn't afford to. Making a long distance call to New York City was an expensive proposition and would cut into their meager profit.

Cecil called his office from the hall phone, which was fortunately disengaged for the moment, but no one answered. He hung up, grumbling, "Where has she gone?"

"I'll let Chief Walker know that you'd like to keep the line open," Lily offered. "But you understand that investigating Mrs. Ethridge's murder is more important right now."

"Of course, of course. But my work is important to me," Cecil said. "Besides, the letter I'm expecting is from a good source, and I have to get my secretary to see how much of my missing manuscript had carbons in the office. I always mean to make a carbon copy, but don't always remember to do so."

"You still haven't found it?"

"I've looked everywhere. The deputy has asked everyone if they've seen it."

"I'm so sorry. I wish I could make it materialize for you."

"If anybody could, it's that lunatic in the basement. What a peculiar young man he is. I can't figure out whether he's brilliant or an idiot."

"Mad Henry?" Lily asked. "A little of both, I think. And he's very rich, so he can indulge himself in all sorts of inventions. Most of which are totally impractical."

Cecil went off, still fretting about his secretary, his manuscript, his stash of carbon copies and life in general. He should never have come here. Meeting his literary idol had been destructive. As much as he liked and admired West's works, especially the early ones, he didn't like the man himself. The grim and sometimes downright vulgar and appalling things he wrote were beautifully done. But coming from him in person, they were merely arrogant. He'd have to be very careful that his final draft of the biography of him didn't reflect his personal distaste.

He stopped on the top step of the second floor, thought for a moment and returned to Mr. Prinney's office. "Chief Walker, might I have another word with you? Have your people thoroughly searched everybody's room?"

"I thought they had," Walker said bitterly. "But I've just found out they didn't even do a decent job on Mrs. Ethridge's room. It's going to take a lot of work on my part to teach them what police work really is at the scene of a crime. Why do you ask?"

"I'm still trying to find my manuscript. I feel quite awkward about asking the other guests and residents if I could search. It's impossibly declassé, really. But I thought maybe your people . . ."

"I'll see what I can do, but I'll stand over them when I get a chance. By the way, Miss Brewster told me you're expecting a telephone call. I've made all my inquiries now and am just waiting for responses, which shouldn't take up as much time."

Cecil went off slightly mollified. He'd take a little nap before dressing for dinner. Maybe he'd dream of where else he might have put the manuscript, though he was ninety-nine percent certain he'd put it on his night table.

Before going upstairs to rest for a short time and dress for dinner, Lily felt compelled to check on a number of things. First was seeing how the dinner preparations were going.

At the early stages of the taking-in-guests plan, Mrs. Prinney had told Lily she intended to do a real Dutch dinner for tonight since a number of local people would be there. This included *haringsalade* and *erwtensoep* for starters, *runderlapjes* and *rode kool* with noodles for the main course and both *ketelkoek met stroopsaus* and *arnhem meisjes* as desserts.

Lily had laughed and said, "Sounds wonderful," then she asked for translations.

"I forget you're not Dutch," Mrs. Prinney said. "*Haringsalade* is what it sounds like, a herring salad. Sliced beets and apples, onions, potatoes, and vinegar with pieces of boned salted herring on top. *Erwtensoep* is pea soup. *Runderlapjes* is stew beef browned in bacon drippings, then stewed in pan juices with vinegar and cloves."

"And *rode kool*?" Lily said, thinking this was the only item she had a chance of pronouncing correctly.

"Cooked cabbage with apples. It's too early for good apples, but I dried quite a few in the fall and will stew them."

"And the desserts?"

"*Ketelkoek met stroopsaus*? Try to guess."

"It sounds like kettle cook. A pudding?"

Mrs. Prinney nodded. "And *met stroopsaus* means with raisins. *Arnhemse meisjes* are puff pastries sprinkled with sugar. It means Arnhem girls. I've never known why, but I suspect it's naughty."

Naturally, Mrs. Prinney had everything under control and just as naturally, Lily's dog Agatha had taken up watch for crumbs in the kitchen. The puff pastries were still at the dough stage on a covered plate sitting over a pan of ice, waiting to be rolled out one last time, cut, and baked in a very hot oven at the last minute. The herring salad was done. ("It has to exchange flavors," Mrs. Prinney said), and the soup had just started bubbling slightly. The stew was simmering gently and filling the kitchen with the scent of cloves.

"This all looks and smells heavenly!" Lily exclaimed. Overcome somewhat, Lily gave her a quick hug. "You're a wonder, Mrs. Prinney."

Mrs. Prinney's face, already red from the heat of the kitchen, got redder. "And so are you, dear."

Lily went next to find out where all her guests were and suggest entertainment if they appeared to be needing it. Bud Carpenter, as well as Rachel and Raymond, were in the library, listening to a musical radio program. Raymond was looking over the bookcases, and Rachel had found a magazine that she was flipping through without much interest. Bud was standing at the French doors, looking outside.

"Bud, where is Mr. West?" Lily asked.

"In his room. Working," Bud said.

Raymond turned and simply glared at Lily, then went back to studying the titles behind the glass doors of the bookcase.

Lily said, "Raymond, I'm sorry to say that we've never found the key to open the doors and read the books."

"It doesn't matter," Raymond said gruffly, his back to her.

"Same to you," Lily muttered under her breath as she left. She felt a fool for letting him kiss her. And then be so rude. She'd been right to begin with when she'd been wary of him resenting her, and apparently he now knew that she'd turned over to Chief Walker the note Lorna had written to him. What had he expected her to do with it? Destroy it for him? Just because she let him kiss her?

She went next to the servants' sitting room in the basement. As she expected, Mad Henry and Robert were down there. Robert was holding a loop of wire and looking very bored while Henry attached it to something on the wall.

"What are you two doing?" she asked.

"God only knows," Robert said. "I'm just the holder and fetcher."

Music suddenly filled the room. "There! It's working again," Henry exclaimed.

"Is that coming from the library?" Lily asked. She moved closer to a box with a speaker on top. She could barely hear voices underneath the music.

"She didn't have to show that stupid note to the cop," Raymond was saying.

Rachel spoke so softly that Lily couldn't understand the words.

"But, Rachel, it's nobody's business how I knew Lorna. It was years ago and not something I want to talk about."

There was more incomprehensible mumbling from Rachel.

Lily felt herself blushing. "Turn it off, Henry. That's eavesdropping and it's not nice." The 'she' that Raymond was talking about was obviously herself and she was embarrassed.

Henry flipped a switch next to the speaker and the music and voices abruptly stopped.

Robert had dropped the bundle of wires he was holding and had a strange expression on his face.

"What is it?" Lily asked.

"Nothing. Just a glimmer of an idea. I'll tell you later."

"Good. I'm too tired to understand anything right now. I'm going to go take a very short nap, if fate will allow it. Don't forget to be in the entry hall to greet the local guests at quarter of seven. Drinks as they arrive, and dinner at seven-thirty. And both of you will be present for drinks and dinner. Understand?"

Lily took hold of Henry's elbow the firm way she remembered her mother doing when she and Robert were children and not paying attention. "Are you listening to me?"

"What? Oh, yes. Yes. I'll be there," Henry said.

As Lily once again passed through the entry hall on her way to the stairs, she saw Phoebe standing by the phone. She had a pad of paper and was furiously writing something. "Yes, I got that. Go on. Yes. I know how to spell it. Continue," she was saying.

Lily, out of sheer curiosity, waited until the phone call was over.

"Whew!" Phoebe said, hanging up. "What a tartar that woman is."

"Who was it?"

"Professor Hoornart's secretary. I told her I didn't know where he was—I'd just come in the door, but I'd look for him if she'd wait. She wouldn't wait and carried on about paying good money for a long distance call. So she made me take down this whole letter she wanted to read to him."

"He'll be glad she finally got it," Lily said. "He's been fretting about it all day."

"Do you know where he is?" Phoebe asked.

"No, but I'll find him. Give me the pad."

"Where's Henry? How's he doing?" Phoebe asked.

"He was interviewed earlier by Chief Walker and told him he'd heard a few things on his call system."

"Like what?"

"Somebody singing. He thought it might have been you."

Phoebe laughed. "I was practicing a song for The Fate."

"And he overheard something about an appendix."

"What kind of appendix?" Phoebe asked, shifting a couple parcels she was carrying.

"The kind in the back of a book. Professor Hoornart's book."

"Thanks for filling me in," Phoebe said. "Henry seems so defenseless. I fret about him a bit. And now I have two dresses to hem for ladies in town and they're picking them up first thing tomorrow. I have to get them done before dinner. I'll be too tired to do a good job later in the evening. Thanks for offering to find Professor Hoornart for me."

Phoebe handed Lily the pad she'd been writing on and hurried up the steps with her two paper-wrapped parcels.

Lily had no idea where Cecil Hoornart had gotten himself to, but she had to get to a sink before she could initiate a long hunt. She'd nibbled on a few things in the kitchen and had sticky hands. She held the pad of paper gingerly, so it wouldn't get sticky as well, and went to her room. She deposited it on her bed and when she came back out of her tiny bathroom, picked it back up to glance at.

Phoebe's handwriting was tiny and neat considering how fast she'd been writing. It was the text of a letter of someone from the town where Julian West had grown up. It started:

"Dear Professor Hoornart, what a lovely letter from you. I'm sorry I couldn't respond as quickly as you might have wished, but I'm having a bit of trouble with my shingles again these days. Anyway, I do remember young Mr. Julian fondly and it has been interesting to cast my mind back and pull my memories forward.

"I was in my twenties when Mr. Julian and Mr. John were children. Mr. John didn't live there then,

of course, but visited often. I was engaged for the
job of being young Mr. Julian's nurse and governess. What a nice child he was. Very bright. He must
have been about four years old, as I recall, and already knew his letters and numbers.

"His father, as you probably know, was the Reverend Ambrose West, a very learned religious
scholar, and I shouldn't have been surprised that
he wished his only son to be taught so young. Reverend West, however, was quite an old man, with
a much younger—and may I be so bold as to say—
rather flighty wife. He also had a growing congre-
gation, and since I was quite well educated, for a
girl, he engaged me to take over young Mr. Julian's
basic education under his direction."

Lily started skimming. It was quite a long note
and Phoebe must have been stuck on the phone for
a considerable time.

The correspondent went on at length about Mr.
Julian's childhood experiences, his hobbies, his several bouts of ill health ("chicken pox with many
spots and later an emergency operation that left
him quite weak for a full month") and her eventual
dismissal ("with a very fine bonus and recommen-
dation letter") when young Mr. Julian was judged
fit and ready to go to a real school five years later.
She then got a job in New Hampshire and rather
lost track of the West family, but heard that the
Good Reverend had died in his bed some five years
after she left the household, and always wondered
if the young wife had remarried.

She closed with effusive thanks for Professor
Hoornart leading her down memory lane this way.
Ever so pleasant those years had been. Her dear
nephew had recently been so kind as to have a tele-

phone installed for her and if Professor Hoornart wished to ask her anything else, he was welcome to call her.

Lily wondered if Cecil would be pleased or disappointed with the letter, and went to look for him.

She ran him to earth in the yellow parlor where he was alone and broodingly nursing a glass of brandy.

"I hope you don't mind that I helped myself," he said listlessly.

"Not a bit," Lily lied. "Your secretary called and Miss Twinkle took a long message for you. Here it is."

With that, he perked up, set down his drink and practically snatched the notes from Lily. "It must have been while I was looking around outside. Thank you so much." He flung himself back on the sofa before the fireplace and started reading, oblivious to Lily's presence.

Lily sighed and went back to her room. Everything was as good as it could be, as far as she could tell. Dinner was well on its way, the guests were accounted for, and she had almost a full hour and a half to herself. Her dog Agatha woofed at the door moments later and Lily let her in.

"Did you get run out of the kitchen?" Lily asked. Agatha wagged her tail.

"Then let's both get a good nap and hope nothing awful happens for a while."

She took off her dress, turned back the bedding and crawled into bed in her slip and was asleep in seconds.

Chapter 17

The most prominent people in town had been invited to the Dutch dinner Mrs. Prinney had prepared. Dr. Polhemus, who always seemed rushed and gabby, said he had a couple of cases pending and would someone please alert him if one of them telephoned.

"Old Mr. Jones keeps taking the splint off his broken arm every time his daughter leaves the house, and I'm worried that Johnny Barker is coming down with another bout of asthma," he volunteered, though no one had asked.

Jack Summer came dressed in a violently checkered suit that he would someday deeply regret purchasing.

Howard Walker, as police chief, had been invited before anything grim had even happened at Grace and Favor, but attended the dinner in the role of active investigator rather than guest, and was trying to overhear everything that was said.

Robert had fretted about serving alcohol. "The old boy Walker replaced didn't mind a bit," he reminded Lily. "He guzzled more than anyone. But

I don't know about Walker. Might he just arrest us on the spot?"

"I'd guess not. Lorna's murder comes first. But you better ask," Lily said. This was something she'd never considered. The house guests had been drinking since they arrived and would expect to go on doing so.

Walker turned out to be mellow, if not entirely disinterested in Prohibition. "If Roosevelt's elected, it'll be over soon anyway," he told Robert, who was greatly relieved.

Lily had also invited two respectable widows who were pillars of the community to the party, just to even out the sexes. They were the ladies who were trying, without much success, to teach Lily how to quilt. Fortunately, they were not offended by drinking alcohol, as Lily knew from the home-made gooseberry wine that was an integral part of the quilting lessons.

Everybody assembled once again in the yellow parlor, but conversation was strained. Julian West took a place on the sofa nearest the fireplace and glared so fiercely at anyone who looked as if he might have approached him, that nobody even sat near him.

When Howard Walker fearlessly sat down on the other end of the sofa, however, West spoke up. "Are you getting anywhere on this murder? I need to go home and get some work done. I shouldn't have come here in the first place. You can't keep us all imprisoned."

"I can, you know," Howard said mildly. "Unless you'd be happier at the town jail? The accommodations aren't nearly as good there and you'd all be rather crowded."

"Jail!" Rachel exclaimed, having overheard. "I can't go to a jail! What would people say?"

Dr. Polhemus called across the room, "Jack, how's that wart on your foot doing?"

"Fine," Jack answered curtly.

"You know, I think I've solved the mystery of warts," Polhemus went on. "One is always the mother wart. If you kill it, you get all the rest of them. I think the wartiest person I ever met was the town butcher. I saw him when he was just a kid. Warts everywhere. I figured out what the mother wart was and you couldn't find a wart on him now if you stripped him naked."

Robert leaned over to Lily and said quietly, "We have to be sure to get a family doctor somewhere else. I wouldn't want Polhemus making small talk about my ailments and warts, if I had any."

"He always talks about his patients," Lily said. "Every time I run into him, he tells me about who he's treating and for what. We'll find somebody in Poughkeepsie or Beacon."

"Or Fishkill. I'd love to have a reason to go to Fishkill from time to time. Just to see who's killing fish."

"Robert, you know perfectly well that 'kill' is Dutch for creek."

Rachel interrupted their conversation. "He isn't *really* going to put us all in a horrible jail, is he? Our parents would have fits. I'd never get out of the house again."

"Never you mind," Robert said. "If he tries to take you to jail, I'll fight him tooth and nail. Besides, he won't. He's just goading Julian West."

"Why would he do that?"

"Because West, like all the rest of us, is a suspect

in Mrs. Ethridge's murder," Robert pointed out.

"Not me," Rachel said. "I didn't even know her."

"But your brother did," Robert said.

Rachel blushed furiously. "He did *not*! I want to go home, Robert. Lily, can't somebody persuade the policeman to let us go home and forget this ever happened?"

"I don't think so," Lily said. "Mrs. Ethridge was murdered. And maybe—probably—someone here did it."

Rachel started sniffling and drew closer to Robert. He patted her hand, looking soulfully into her eyes.

Dear God, Lily thought, *he isn't falling for her, is he? I couldn't bear to have this silly girl as a sister-in-law.*

"I think dinner is almost ready," she said to the group. "I haven't put out place cards, so you're welcome to sit wherever you like."

The already huge dining room table had three more extensions put in and somehow Mrs. Prinney had unearthed a lovely ivory damask tablecloth to fit and even had matching napkins at each place.

Lily often wondered where she found these things that she always seemed to have at hand. Was there some huge secret storeroom in the mansion that Lily herself had not yet come across? It was certainly possible.

Toward each end of the table, there were large, low crystal bowls full of wild flowers that Mimi had gathered in the woods. The ancient silverware with the elaborate engraved "B" on the handles was brilliantly polished. The blue and white china that Mrs. Prinney said had actually come from China when Miss Flora Brewster was a girl and still had hopes of marrying, was lovely with its little Chinese scenery painted under the glaze. It was altogether a beautiful table setting.

Everybody jockeyed for a place at the table. Most tried to get as far as possible from Julian West because he was being so surly, but Jack Summer and Dr. Polhemus took the opposite view and flanked him.

Jack wanted an interview, at least an informal one. And Dr. Polhemus was determined to find out about the variety of war injuries West had seen. He apparently had no concept that this wasn't suitable table talk. When Lily noticed that even Addie, who was sitting directly across from West, was getting pale, Lily finally had to ask Robert, to her left, to make an excuse to pull the doctor away from the table and explain to him that war wounds didn't go with dinner.

"I can't tell him what to talk about," Robert said.

As a diversion, Lily asked Mrs. Prinney to explain to the guests about the dinner. Mrs. Prinney was delighted to do so, reporting that her people had come from Amsterdam nearly two hundred years ago, and the recipes had been handed down each generation from mother to daughters.

"Excellent food, Dutch," Dr. Polhemus said, tucking into his *haringsalade*. "My mother always cooked this way, but not as well as Mrs. Prinney, I must admit."

Lily and Robert exchanged a relieved glance. Robert winked.

He took charge of keeping everyone off unpleasant subjects. He asked Jack about the circulation of the *Voorburg-on-Hudson Times*, and Jack got to brag about the increased subscriptions and how he had to rehire two of the delivery boys who had been let go during the former editor's tenure. When the conversation about several recent articles started to lag, Robert asked the ladies from town about whether they'd be displaying their quilts at the fête tomorrow.

This got them to the main course.

When dessert was served, Robert gave the men a turn to talk about sports they enjoyed, which didn't turn out well because many of them were hunters and the stories threatened to veer toward the bloody. He switched to what everybody's favorite radio programs were, and dessert was saved.

Lily was grateful to him for attempting to keep the conversations light and amusing. An outsider would have never guessed that there'd been a murder in this very home less than a day before. She glanced at Howard Walker. He'd been very quiet, merely an observer, and had made no attempt to bring up the topic. He met her gaze and smiled. She nodded her thanks.

As Mimi and Bud Carpenter passed around the table with coffee and tea, Robert stood up. "I suppose it isn't appropriate to toast with a coffee cup, but my sister and our maid Mimi have done a wonderful job and Mrs. Prinney has provided us with the best meal I've ever had." He tapped his fragile coffee cup against Cecil's cup, which Cecil was just raising to his lips.

"Here's to the ladies!" Robert said.

There was giggling and blushing and Lily and Mrs. Prinney almost got teary. Lily soon "gathered eyes" and the women departed the dining room to leave the men to their port. As usual, most of the women scattered to repair their hair and shake the wrinkles out of their frocks.

The plan for the evening was games. Robert excused himself from the men in the dining room and set up some extra tables in the yellow parlor. He set out decks of cards for bridge on two tables, and a pachisi board, dice and tokens on a third. If people didn't want to play anything, they could just chat. And later, there was a dance music broadcast on the radio. He had brought the radio from the library to the parlor. Last night had been formal with place cards and a lecture from Julian West. This evening was to be friendly and familylike.

Only Mr. Prinney excused himself from the gathering. "I have a lot of work to do and Chief Walker has taken over my office for most of the day," he told Lily.

He looked tired and older than usual, Lily thought. "You have no obligation to entertain the guests," she said. "That's Robert's job and mine."

The two respectable widows who quilted were also cutthroat bridge players and insisted that Phoebe and Lily make up a foursome. Addie sat by herself, glancing through a book. Bud Carpenter stood quietly by the door, being the perfect servant. Robert, Rachel, Mad Henry and Raymond played pachisi. Mad Henry lost round after round, because he was making notes of the frequency of the combinations of the dice. No doubt to produce better dice, Lily speculated. Julian had resumed his solitary place on the sofa.

Lily was feeling terribly smug. It was a good party in spite of the fact that one of the guests was now lying in the town funeral parlor. She wouldn't have thought it was possible.

She didn't notice that Howard Walker had once again sat down by Julian West. Then, suddenly, as Lily was about to play a three of hearts, all hell broke loose.

"You bastard!" West shouted at Walker. "Leave me alone. I had nothing to do with that woman's death. I hardly remembered her. Just ask Bud. He keeps an eye on me like a mother eagle with a chick, damn the man."

"Mr. West—" Walker started to say.

"I swear to God if I get up in the night to take a piss, there's Bud outside the bathroom door asking if I'm all right. I didn't leave my room all night. Just ask him."

Walker turned to Bud Carpenter, who was looking unconcerned with the Great Man's outburst.

"Is this true?"

"Yes. Absolutely true, sir. The Captain went to his room and stayed there all night. I would have known otherwise. I'm a very light sleeper . . . sir." He added the last word grudgingly.

The ladies playing bridge with Lily were ignoring the shouting, but Lily was upset. "Could you take this conversation somewhere else?" she asked.

She was ignored. West was well under steam now and had a few more things to say while he was at it. "Why don't you go after that woman?" He pointed at Addie. "I hear she had quite a history with Mrs. Ethridge. She stole her boyfriend or some stupid thing."

Addie threw down her book and said, "How dare you!"

"And she'd written a letter to Raymond Cameron. A very personal letter, I hear."

Raymond's face turned puce, but he didn't shout. "I didn't know Mrs. Ethridge."

"You never met her?" Walker asked. "Never even heard her name?"

"I suppose I'd heard the name," Raymond said, off-guard. "I believe she might have been a client of my Uncle Joe, who was a lawyer. I worked in his office one summer. I might have seen the name there."

"We'll talk more about this later," Walker said, standing up. "It seems as though an awful lot of eavesdropping has gone on here."

Chapter 18

Robert was so angry he couldn't sleep that night. Everything had been going so swimmingly well. Then Walker had to go off half-cocked and question West at a purely social occasion and ruin everything. Poor Lily. She'd worked so hard at this whole project of having congenial paying guests and a celebrity guest. The celebrity was an ass. And one of the paying guests was dead, probably at the hand of another of the guests.

In fairness, he couldn't genuinely fault Howard Walker. He was supposed to have been at Grace and Favor as an honored local guest originally. It wasn't his fault Mrs. Ethridge had gone and gotten her silly self killed and Walker had to wear his professional hat.

But Julian West was beyond the pale. What an ugly, outrageous performance he'd put on. Unfortunately, it seemed to clear him of guilt. That was a shame. He'd been Robert's favorite suspect for the murder.

Robert got out of bed finally, put on his dressing gown, which was getting tatty, but these days new silk dressing gowns weren't in his plans. He went prowling. The only person likely to be awake and about was Mad Henry. And sure as anything, he'd be down in the servants' quarters fooling about with his calling system. And so Henry was. But he'd fallen asleep in a wooden chair with his head on the servants' dining table. There was a faint jumble of sounds coming from the speaker.

Robert listened for a bit. Mostly, it seemed to be people snoring.

"Henry, wake up."

Henry sprung to life. He must have been as light a sleeper as Bud Carpenter claimed to be.

"You did what I asked?"

"Yes. It was easy. Each box has a switch that works three ways. Talk, listen and off. I set them all for talk when that military guy started going off his head. I figured nobody would miss me."

"So if everybody is talking to someone, you'll hear them all at once."

Henry nodded. "And probably not understand a word anyone says. That isn't the purpose of the system."

"It wasn't your purpose," Robert amended. "Go to bed, Henry. I just want to listen awhile. Walker said there had been a lot of eavesdropping. He doesn't know what real eavesdropping is. They can't hear us, can they?" he said, dropping his voice to a whisper.

"No. Talk. Listen. Off. Can't be two at a time."

Henry was bored with listening to snoring and left to get some genuine horizontal sleep.

Robert was soon bored nearly senseless, too. He'd almost nodded off when he heard real voices. They were faint and scratchy and almost incomprehensible. Two people seemed to be moving around in one of the rooms. As they approached the gadget, the voices got louder and faded as they got farther away.

"If only (mumble, mumble) about that damned appendix," a male voice said. The sound quality was too bad to be sure whose it was.

The other person responded, "But . . ." and there was a burst of static that wiped out the words. Or maybe it was the same person in a different tone of voice.

Suddenly Agatha barked very loudly right in Robert's ear. He reeled back in shock. Then he heard Lily (he supposed) say sleepily, "Oh, Agatha, go back to sleep."

Agatha mumbled.

There were no further sounds except snoring—Agatha's loudest of all. She must have been sleeping right next to the speaker.

Robert found a button that turned down the sound and went back to his room very quietly. None of the doors along the second floor hall seemed to quite meet the floor perfectly, and in the dead of night, you could see slivers of yellow if lights were on in the rooms. But all was dark. He checked the third floor where only Phoebe and Cecil had rooms. Complete darkness there, too. He went to his own room and stood deep in thought.

So who had he heard? Cecil had talked about wanting to do an appendix to his book on Julian West. If it had been West and Bud speaking, West might have been expressing irritation at having his life pried into and being expected to remember dates and places.

If the words had come from Cecil's room, who could he have been talking to? Himself, maybe?

People sometimes did that. Robert had caught himself at it from time to time. Maybe it was all one voice. Cecil could have been lamenting to himself that if he hadn't asked so many personal questions, rather than sticking to West's books, they might have gotten along better.

So much for eavesdropping. Robert hung up his dressing gown and fell into bed.

The fête was to start at ten. People were in the yard setting up and yelling back and forth at each other at seven. Elgin Prinney rolled onto his back with a groan and said, "Emmaline, we should have slept in a room on the other side of the house. Emmaline? Where are you?"

The next thing he heard was her voice out in the yard. "No, Paulette. Not there. Over here." Paulette was the town butcher's simple-minded girl who occasionally helped in the kitchen. If she was only given one job to do, and it was done for her as an example, she was a good worker. But why did Emmaline have to bellow at her that way so early in the morning?

Elgin groaned again as he hauled himself out of bed. He'd been such a spritely young man, and hated that he was getting old. Everybody must feel that way at his age. But it hadn't slowed Emmaline down. Nor did the people in their fifties who'd come here this weekend seem to feel a sense of aging.

Julian West was as energetic and rude as a twenty-year-old. And a showoff to boot. Had West been younger and less famous, Elgin would have told him to shut his mouth five or six times already.

And Lorna Ethridge surely didn't acknowledge her age. But then, she'd never get any older.

Elgin made a trip to the bathroom and came back to sit on the edge of the bed again, getting his wits about him before dressing. Lorna Ethridge. She'd been an attractive woman. Just the right degree of plumpness. She had lovely eyes and small feminine hands, and dressed well. It was a shame she hadn't been as good a woman as she had looked. Elgin didn't subscribe to theories of mysterious outsiders following her to Voorburg-on-Hudson and thence to Grace and Favor Cottage.

She had been murdered, he felt, by someone in the house. Granted, the family (he had come to think of himself and Emmaline as family with Lily and Robert) wasn't very good about locking up all the many doors of the mansion. Some, in fact, had no keys and were either permanently locked or unlocked. But that didn't mean that a stranger had pursued Mrs. Ethridge here. She had turned up under false pretenses for motives of her own. Who could guess what they were?

Was she trying to reinstate a former relationship with Julian West? He was only slightly older than she, or at least he looked it, no doubt rich, and very famous. An appealing catch for a woman whose range of likely husbands was diminishing. Hadn't he heard from someone that she'd been married and widowed several times? Or was that just his impression?

And what on earth was that business of the note to Raymond Cameron? Another man she was after? Surely not. She was nearly old enough to be his mother. Certainly she couldn't have caught him in her net. Maybe she was trying to blackmail him about something. But what secrets could a vapid young man like that have?

And there was Lily's dear friend Addie Jonson. She had a motive, he had to admit against his better wishes. Lily adored Addie, and he hoped it wasn't she. But a woman scorned—especially a woman scorned for another woman, and an older, more beautiful woman at that—could be a powerful force. However, if Addie were given to murderous rages, wouldn't she have acted on them before this? Apparently her betrothed's rejection of her for Lorna Ethridge had happened years ago and they had gone on living in the same town for some time.

If Addie Jonson *were* the perpetrator of this dastardly crime, what had lit the fuse at long last? He tried to cast his mind back to the various gatherings and departings during the last two days. He'd never seen them exchanging words—heated or otherwise. Then again, he'd not thought there was reason to keep tabs on them. Or anyone else for that matter. Perhaps they'd had private words in Mrs. Ethridge's room after dinner the night before last. The rooms did connect through a hall. Nobody would have seen Addie going into Mrs. Ethridge's room. Addie certainly had the safest access to the woman.

"Mr. Prinney," Emmaline Prinney called up to him from the yard. She always called him Mr. Prinney in public. "You need to get stirring yourself."

I do, indeed, he said to himself. And Walker needed to spread his investigation farther. Elgin himself realized he'd been thinking along unfamiliar lines. He was thinking about sex and passion.

Words he would never say out loud. But the murder might not be about either.

Howard Walker felt as old and tired as Mr. Prinney did this morning. He simply wasn't getting anywhere. This was his first important criminal investigation and he was disappointed in himself. Lord knew he'd knocked around the state long enough to know about the full range of human nature.

He'd been a wild kid, sensitive and belligerent about his Indian looks, even though he had only a tiny sliver of Indian heritage. His parents had been poor long before everyone else got poor and he'd fallen in with the wrong crowd when he was fourteen. He'd seen crime and criminals from the other side, until his mother found out and took him by the ear and walloped him good.

And he'd gone to school with upper-class people when he got his two years of college by secretly working at an ice cream stand when he wasn't in classes. He was now firmly in the middle class and on equal footing with the people of Voorburg. But all that experience wasn't serving him well.

Mr. Prinney went to his office downstairs with the intention of calling Walker at home, but found the man sitting in his office already. Or still. "Have you been here all night?"

"Thought I should be. I took a look around the house every hour and napped in a room Miss Brewster had made up for me between times."

"That's taking your job rather too seriously, isn't it?"

Mr. Prinney was glad when Walker took offense.

"It's impossible to take murder lightly," Walker said.

"I've been thinking about this," Mr. Prinney said. "And all wrong, I believe."

Walker leaned forward and looked at him intently. "What do you mean?"

"I was considering Mrs. Ethridge's—let us say—allure. She was a most attractive woman. But in my experience money is the key to most crimes. Of course, I'm a property attorney, so my view may be skewed. But I've had clients who came to blows over their grandmother's little nest egg when it didn't amount to a hill of beans."

Walker leaned back in Mr. Prinney's chair. "Money . . ." he said thoughtfully.

"Blackmail money more specifically. It crossed my mind this morning that the murderer wasn't the only one with a motive. Mrs. Ethridge came here for a reason and I think you should find out what it was."

Howard Walker got out his notebook and licked his pencil. "Talk."

Chapter 19

The fête got going earlier than it was supposed to. The backyard of Grace and Favor was full of about two dozen townspeople either setting up games and tables or looking over the preparations.

Lily and Robert roamed around among them, introducing themselves to those they hadn t met and chatting with those they knew. About half the people greeted them cordially. A few were obnoxiously friendly and the remainder were a little stand-offish.

In a brief quiet moment, Lily said, "I wonder how they'd all react if they knew we're as poor as most of them are these days."

"Probably the same," Robert said. "The really chummy ones would quit being so chummy. But the rest would still regard us as strangers. I think you have to have lived here for quite a few generations before you count as really 'local.'"

Lily nodded. "It was the same before the Crash in the circles we moved in. It wasn't enough to have money. It had to be very old money to count socially. You could always recognize the new money people because they dressed too well and spent too much and talked about money too often. And we treated them like 'newcomers.' Expecting them to prove themselves worthy of our company. What snobs we were."

"Everybody's snobby about their 'own kind,' I think. Still, we ought to be getting some credit here for being a distant part of a family that's been around Voorburg for ages," Robert said. "Maybe more people will warm up to us eventually. At least nobody's been openly hostile."

They went down on the long, lush lawn that overlooked the river. Men were laying out lanes for foot races by pouring crushed lime from the spout of a galvanized can. A big group of children, mostly boys and a few tomboyish girls, were practicing running and shrieking with glee.

A few families had laid out quilts on the grass, and the husbands were napping while the wives visited with neighbors. A horseshoe pitching field was being assembled. Some of the young girls could be seen flitting around woods next to the lawn picking wild flowers to put in their hair or to make daisy chains.

Robert looked around and said, "Lily, I hate to admit this, and will deny I ever said it if you ever tell any of our old friends, but today I really like living here. I thought it was going to be so dull in the country. But today proves it sometimes isn't. Just today, nobody's thinking about the economy or where the next job or meal is coming from."

Lily took his arm. "I like it almost all of the time. But I always liked staying at our houses away from the City better than being in the middle of society's pressures. You thrived on that. I do hope we'll eventually make real friends here."

"We have. Mr. and Mrs. Prinney. Jack Summer. Chief Walker."

"But only the Prinneys know our true situation. If you aren't honest with people, you can't consider them friends."

"We could wear breadboards saying, 'Once rich, now poor,'" Robert said.

Lily laughed and said, "I'm still too much of a snob. Every now and then I get a furious itch to put on my best clothes and go to a real debutante ball with all the glitter and silliness."

Robert shuddered. "Euww. I hope the urge to cavort about with debutantes is something that passes off quickly. Some of my most hideous memories are debs dances. Girls who were spotty and coltish six months earlier queening it over their little sisters and wearing far too much of their mothers' jewelry."

They greeted a few more of the townspeople down by the bench where Lily and Robert often sat and watched the river traffic pass by, and then headed back to the heart of the fête nearer the mansion.

The town butcher had started a fire in a pit that the brother and sister had always wondered about the purpose of, and was cooking big marvelous-smelling sausages on sticks to sell. A farmer from just outside town was offering glasses of buttermilk and his wife was busy running down the empty glasses and recovering them to be rinsed out for reuse. The quilting society ladies were using the clothesline to display their best quilts, which were spectacular.

Children had brought cats and dogs and piglets and rabbits to show off for the pet show. Robert went around complimenting the children and stroking the pets, all except the piglets.

"If I get through without ever touching a live pig, I will consider it a life well lived," he muttered to Lily.

Some of the ladies of town who kept vegetable gardens—as almost all did these days—were selling or giving away their extra canned beans, tomatoes and onions. Others had afghans and hand-knitted hats and gloves and shawls to sell.

Few people had extra money to purchase these items, and everyone knew it, but part of the point was simply to show off good work. A quart of green beans laid in the bottle in an elaborate wickerworklike pattern, or a baby blanket with exceptionally fine knitting, was a mark that they hadn't let down their standards and wouldn't do so no matter how tough times got.

And the crowd that had turned out early continued to grow. It seemed that virtually the entire town had shown up. Perhaps some of them had even come from nearby towns. Many called each other "aunt" and "uncle" and "cousin," even if the blood relationships were distant. This made Lily sad. She'd lost her parents, and was no longer the social peer of most of her cousins who were too far flung to run into at a party. She had misplaced Robert in the crowd and looked for him.

Instead, she spotted Cecil Hoornart wandering around, looking bemused.

"Are you enjoying this?" Lily asked.

"It certainly is something you'd never see in the City. Where did all these people come from?"

Lily shrugged. "I have no idea. Robert and I are newcomers and hardly know any more of these people than you do. I recognize the butcher, the greengrocer and the librarian, and the lady with the pincurl hair without the pins is Mr. Prinney's secretary."

"That's frightening hair, isn't it?" Cecil said with a laugh.

"You're feeling happier today, aren't you?"

"I got back to my secretary and she does have at least half the book on carbons," he said. "I'm still upset about the good copy, but I haven't lost everything. But I'm still convinced that someone stole it and disposed of it and that worries me. It had to be West. Who else would be interested?"

"Lorna Ethridge? Maybe she thought you'd put something unflattering about her in it."

"How could I have? I'd never heard of her."

"But she told Addie she'd been engaged to Julian West. If it was true, and if she thought you knew it and might name her in your book as his jilted lover . . . ?"

"I don't see how she'd have had time after that first night's dinner. We rejoined the ladies quite soon after it. How could she have taken it and so thoroughly hidden it so quickly? Unless she took it while I was interviewing West? And even if I had known about their engagement, if there ever was one, I probably wouldn't mention the woman's name unless she was a prominent individual."

"But she wouldn't have known that either. I'm not convinced she's the thief, it's just a possibility."

"What about Bud? He'd do it if West told him to," Cecil said.

Lily laughed at this. "Bud is the boss of that pair. West only acts like he's the master by being rude.

I don't think Bud Carpenter would do a thing he didn't want to do."

Cecil smiled. "I think you're right. And I don't think he knows or cares about books of any kind. I tried to engage him in a conversation of what he liked to read and he huffed up and said he didn't have time for reading. He was a busy man. As if I'm not. He's probably illiterate anyway. You don't think there might have been a reason for any of the others—the Cameron brother and sister, or your friend Miss Jonson—to take it, do you?"

"I see no reason why anyone would take it, really. Everybody would have probably assumed you'd made a carbon copy instead of taking it away from your office without the copy locked up safely. If I were a writer, I think I'd buy a safe to put copies in. But then, I'm not a writer and maybe it's easier to reconstruct your book than I suppose."

"No, it'll be difficult. But I have the chapters organized and titled, and that and my notes will probably help replace the missing parts. But I have learned a hard lesson from this."

A little boy tore by them at that moment and dropped a baseball he'd been playing with. Cecil picked it up and when the boy turned to see where it had gone, Cecil lobbed it to the child quite expertly. Lily was surprised that an academic like Cecil had ever played ball enough to have a good arm. He was so portly, so tweedy, so indoors-pale and professorial-looking that she couldn't imagine he'd ever played ball in his life.

"Good throw," Phoebe Twinkle said, coming up behind Cecil and Lily. "Professor Hoornart, have you seen the quilts? You must come and look at them closely. The handwork is superb. And you might want to buy some of the canned vegetables to give your friends in town as gifts. They're beautiful, too."

Cecil was flattered and went away with Phoebe with excuses to Lily.

"Please, please, go enjoy yourself," Lily said. "That's the whole reason for this day."

She roamed around, chatting with people and checking on whether all her guests were present or accounted for. It might be a little too easy for one of them to make a quiet exit with all the milling around. Perhaps some of these unfamiliar people had been brought in by Walker with the same concern in mind.

She found Rachel surrounded by a bunch of young men from the village who were impressed with her big-city good looks, but unable to find anything to talk to her about except cars, cows and local gossip about hunting accidents. Rachel looked desperate.

Lily took pity on her. "Rachel, I'm sorry to interrupt, but I need to talk to you in the house for a moment."

Rachel looked panicked, apparently thinking it might be yet another interview with Walker.

As they walked toward the mansion, Lily said quietly, "I don't need you for anything. I was just performing a rescue mission. You looked a little overwhelmed."

"Oh, thank you!" Rachel said, taking refuge inside anyway.

When Lily located Raymond, he was sitting in a deck chair someone else must have brought along and looking like he might fall asleep any moment.

He didn't need saving and she didn't bother to speak to him.

Bud Carpenter was standing around watching the horseshoe pitch. He was smiling slightly and looking utterly relaxed for the first time since he'd arrived. He had his hands behind his back and his posture gave him a bit of pot belly instead of his usual rigid military bearing. Lily thought it was rather funny and wondered if he might be one of those men who wore a corset when he was on duty.

Julian West was simply wandering around. He obviously didn't want to make conversation with the locals, not that many of them would recognize him anyway. He looked angry. Whether he was still chafing at being considered a suspect in Lorna's death or disappointed at not being recognized as someone of importance was anybody's guess.

Lily finally spotted Henry going toward the woods with a leather satchel. Now, why would he be doing that? Surely he wasn't going to hook up his loony call system in the woods. Lily hurried to catch up with him.

"Henry, hold up. What are you doing?"

"I'm going to check tree rings."

"What?"

"I bought a gadget about two years ago that allows you to take a core sample from a tree just like with a core sample of a rock strata. I've never had a chance to try it out."

He rummaged in his satchel and held out the tool for her inspection.

"But why would you want to do that?"

He looked surprised. "Just out of curiosity," he

said as if it were the obvious answer to a very fool-
ish question.

"Have fun," Lily said, knowing she was wasting
sarcasm on him.

Chapter 20

The fête went on all day long. It lost a bit of the verve after lunch when most everyone who could afford to buy food or had brought it along had a full stomach and needed to rest awhile. Some of the invited guests at Grace and Favor came inside to take naps and others came indoors briefly to partake of a light luncheon of cold cuts and bread that Mrs. Prinney had put out for them.

But by three P.M. the fête was under full steam again. There were foot races, three-legged races, even baby races, which were hysterically funny because the babies didn't get the point and went crawling off every which way.

There were jump rope contests for the older girls, marble shooting contests for the boys, wrestling matches and even a short marching demonstration by the veterans in the afternoon, which Julian West watched sadly.

As evening came on, banjos and fiddles were brought out and the music and dancing started. This was commenced by the lone Scotsman from the town playing as lively a tune as possible on his bagpipes. This was apparently the traditional opening to the evening activities.

When the sun started setting, kerosene lanterns were set up on tables where children couldn't get near them and a space was cleared on the lawn for dancing.

As Lily moved through the crowd, she could smell beer and whiskey from time to time. *So much for Prohibition*, she thought.

To Lily's surprise, Phoebe Twinkle was one of the featured singers. She had a strong soprano voice and a vast repetoire of country songs. Most of the dances were country dances. Lines and circles of people exchanging places in elaborate patterns. As many children as adults participated. Skirts spinning, feet stomping, encouraging yelps were the order of the evening. A small proportion of those whose religious beliefs or energy levels prohibited dancing nevertheless watched with smiles, and some clapped to the music.

After a while, babies were nursed and put to sleep on quilts in the area closest to the kitchen where they wouldn't be stepped on. Mr. and Mrs. Prinney set up chairs nearby and served as baby-watchers.

Young couples furtively crept away into the woods. Some were dragged back by vigilant parents or grandparents.

Lily was fascinated and deeply touched by how much entertainment small town people could have without money. Parties in her "old world" had involved hired dance bands, haughty-looking professional waiters, expensive fancy food which most people merely picked at, men in tuxes and women in now unimaginably costly dresses and jewels, and a rather unhealthy sense of social competition instead of physical feats.

"Are you enjoying yourself?" Robert asked as he found her still watching the dancers much later.

"Enormously. Shall we try dancing?"

"We'd just mess up the pattern."

"I'll bet they'd forgive us and if they don't, we'll stop. We used to be pretty good dancers, both of us."

"But not *this* kind of dancing," Robert objected.

"Well, I don't mind making a fool of myself to learn," Lily said. "We live here now, we better make ourselves a part of it."

"Then we better find good, patient partners. I'll ask Phoebe to help me. And you can ask—oh, my goodness!"

Robert goggled as Cecil Hoornart, in fine fettle, pranced by them, perfectly in step.

"Well, if he can do it, so can I!" Robert exclaimed.

Lily located Jack Summer, who had discarded his horrible checked suit jacket, and asked him to help her learn the steps. A half hour later, she was sweating, out of breath, and very happy with her newfound dance skills. She'd galloped up and down the center row with half the men in town, locked elbows with them and been swung violently around in dizzying circles and only tripped up on the patterns three times. The music and the clapping were heady incentives.

She went inside and splashed water on her face in the kitchen sink to cool off. Most of the other dancers were also taking a rest and the music changed. Ballads and old-fashioned laments were being sung. Mr. Prinney had given up for the evening and Lily sat quietly with Mrs. Prinney and the sleeping babies.

"Have you enjoyed yourself, dear?" Mrs. Prinney asked.

"Oh, yes."

"I met Mr. Prinney at a Fate, you know," she said, pronouncing it as the locals did. "I was a slim girl then if you can believe it, and a fine dancer. I wore my best pink dress that year and it was the first time he'd noticed me. We married six months later."

"How nice," Lily murmured. She was so tired she was on the brink of falling asleep. "This is the first time I've really felt that I'm part of Voorburg. That people just accepted me as a neighbor."

"The Fate does that to people," Mrs. Prinney said softly, stifling a yawn.

Young women were starting to come to gather up their babies and Lily helped them for a while before going inside. She wanted more than anything to take a quick bath and go to bed, but as hostess she had duties to perform before she could indulge herself.

She went from room to room slipping cards under bedroom doors that gave the menus, times of meals and possible activities for the next day. It was supposed to have been the last full day, but she feared she'd be stuck with a houseful of guests who would have to be fed while Howard Walker continued his questioning.

She really wanted more than anything for them all to leave, so she could sleep soundly for two days, then count up the profits. Next time they tried this, *if* they did it again, she wouldn't let herself get so weary before anyone arrived.

As she left the notes, she tapped on the doors, taking "roll" once more. Bud Carpenter answered the door and she caught a glimpse of Julian West crossing the room in his stocking feet.

Rachel was already in her nightclothes with cold cream on her face and looked clownish. Too bad Robert wasn't around to see her this way.

When she tapped on Raymond's door, he called out, "Who's there?" suspiciously and she merely slid his note under the door.

The music from outdoors faded to merely one banjo and she could hear automobile doors slamming and motors starting up. She went to Cecil's room and received no response. Thinking he might have fallen into a deep sleep after his exertions on the lawn, she peeked in the door. No sign of him. That was worrisome.

But as she headed back down the stairs, she met him limping up them.

"I was looking for you," she said.

Cecil winced. "I haven't gotten that much exercise in one day for the last ten years at least. I seriously considered crawling up the stairs instead of trying to walk."

"Where did you learn to dance that way?" Lily asked.

"I grew up spending summers with my grandmother in Virginia. They do a lot of dancing in Virginia."

Lily handed him his note and remembered something she'd meant to discuss with him earlier. "Have you told anyone but me about your secretary having so much of your manuscript in carbons?"

"No, I don't think so. Maybe I mentioned it to Miss Twinkle."

"If you don't mind my advice, I'd suggest you keep it to yourself," Lily said.

"Why?"

"I'm not sure. It's just that it appears that someone stole the original for some reason—"

"—and might try to steal the carbons," Cecil finished her sentence. "Very sensible of you, Miss Brewster. That should have occurred to me as well."

"And have you see Robert, Phoebe or Mad Henry?"

"I passed Robert in the kitchen. And Phoebe was helping Mrs. Prinney pass out the last of the babies when I came in. I haven't seen Henry for hours."

Henry wasn't in his room. He wasn't in the yellow parlor. He wasn't in the kitchen with Robert.

"He's probably in the basement again," Robert said through a jelly sandwich he was polishing off. He yelled down the steps, but there was no answer. Lily went down and the basement was dark and silent. She turned on the light to be sure, but Henry wasn't there.

"I'm worried," she told Robert when she came back up.

"I am, too," Robert said, gulping down the last of his sandwich. "I'll find Howard Walker. He must have had people watching all of us."

Howard Walker wasn't happy to hear that Henry was missing. He called a couple of his "watchers" over and it appeared that nobody admitted to having been assigned to keep an eye on Henry in particular.

"Miss Brewster, will you ask all the women in your household, and Mr. Brewster the men, when they last saw him?" Walker asked. "I'll ask the townsfolk who are still around."

The result was dissatisfying. Nobody had paid much attention to Henry all day. Raymond and Rachel both claimed they'd seen so little of him before that they'd forgotten that he was even a guest or just what he looked like. Julian West just grumbled that he had better things to think about and Bud said the last time he'd seen him was just after breakfast.

Phoebe had actually kept an eye out for him, but saw him last inside Grace and Favor in the morning. Mimi hadn't bothered to wonder about him, but when questioned carefully said she didn't recall him coming inside to eat anytime. Since she was largely responsible for keeping the food fresh and available, this was bad news, too.

It seemed, when everyone was questioned, that Lily herself had probably been the last to have run into him. She recounted to Chief Walker how she had questioned him about the tools he was carrying around and he'd said something about tree rings and went off into the woods.

"And you didn't see him come back out? Well, we'll have to have a search. Find all the flashlights you can and I'll get all the men who are still here to search."

"I'll roust Agatha and let her smell some of his clothes," Robert suggested. "Maybe she could find him by scent."

"You don't really think something awful has happened to him?" Lily asked.

Walker just looked at her, then turned and started organizing a search of the woods around Grace and Favor.

Chapter 21

Nearly everyone got involved in the hunt for Henry.

Men from the village who hadn't yet left the grounds, most of the men at Grace and Favor, Walker and his deputies. Flashlights were handed out and when the batteries died, kerosene lamps were dragged out of the basement and garage and used.

The only man who refused to help was Raymond, who said, with a fine combination of cowardice and common sense, that if there was a killer or kidnapper among the searchers he didn't want to offer himself up as another victim. He didn't even have the grace to be embarrassed when Addie took his place.

How could I have thought he was a decent man? Lily chided herself.

Lily, Mimi and Mrs. Prinney made up sandwiches and Mrs. Prinney turned up a gallon or two of apple cider to warm and spice. Rachel wasn't any more interested than her brother in participating and stayed in her room.

"Maybe we'll find the Lindbergh baby and his

kidnapper while we're at it," Robert said with grim humor. "Nobody's found him yet."

Walker assigned Bud Carpenter, Julian West and Addie Jonson to search nearest the house because none of them was familiar with the area and they could get lost themselves. The local people were assigned to the various paths that went through the woods. Each would search both sides of the path. It was a large area and quite dark.

They were at it for hours. In spite of Howard Walker's instructions, the searchers kept running into one another in the woods and frightening one another half to death.

Men came back for fortifying food and drink and went back out again. "He might not even be out there. Somebody might have nabbed him and taken him away, like that poor little baby in New Jersey," one of them said, unconsciously echoing Robert.

"Or he might have just driven off," another said. "Has anybody checked how he got here?"

"Walker said he drove a little truck," the first man said. "It's still here."

"Then maybe he found himself on a road and got a ride. He could be on his way back right now."

"Wassamatter with you? The guy's in the woods somewhere."

"My wife's gonna kill me for being so late getting home. Wish we could afford a telephone."

It was Robert who found Henry. Agatha had been no help whatsoever and gone running off after a rabbit. Robert raised a great shout and men came crashing through the woods toward him. Henry was on his side, tied up with thin ropes.

"Is he alive?" Walker, the first to arrive, asked.

Robert had turned Henry on his back and put his head on Henry's chest. "Quiet. Yes. His heart's beating. Help me get him untied."

"Wait a second. Let me get a good look at these ropes."

"Hurry up. We've got to get him to a hospital. Why do you want to look at the damned ropes?"

"I've got an ambulance waiting, just in case. Look, the ropes on his hands are secure. The ones on his feet are just looped around loosely."

"What difference does it make?" Robert started trying to untie Henry's hands.

Agatha came tearing back with a clump of fur at the edge of her mouth and a scratch on her nose. She crowded in next to Robert as if wanting to help. He shoved her away.

"It could mean the person who did this was interrupted and didn't get to finish the job."

"Killing him, you mean?"

Walker nodded. "Don't bother with his hands. He can be untied in the ambulance."

Several other men had arrived during this conversation. One had a canvas tarp, which had once done duty as a sail, and they'd picked up a couple broken tree limbs to make a primitive stretcher. Walker, who had the only flashlight that still functioned, led the way and Robert brought up the back.

"I want to go with him," Robert said.

"We'll follow in my car," Walker told him. "You'd just be in the way in the ambulance."

The women inside heard the whoops outside as word was passed along that Henry had been found, and Lily ran to tell the ambulance driver to pull around to the back of the house regardless of the lawn.

Lily took one quick, shocked look at Henry and asked Robert, "Is he dead?"

"Not quite. We're taking him to Poughkeepsie to the hospital there. There's only Dr. Polhemus and his office here in Voorburg. Get everybody out of the way."

Lily shooed people out of the path of the ambulance, which took off so fast when Henry had been popped into the back with the assistant that it gouged a hole in the grass. Robert had insisted that he and Walker take the Duesie and he was honking the horn in front of the house to summon the police chief. They, too, took off like a shot.

On a straight, empty stretch of Route 9, Robert overtook the ambulance and they arrived in Poughkeepsie first. He and Walker were standing outside when the ambulance arrived.

"He's doing okay, I think," the attendant said. "Started to mumble when I took the ropes off his hands." They hauled Henry into the hospital.

Robert went to the open door of the ambulance and brought the ropes into the light at the front door. "I recognize these."

"From where?" Walker asked.

"They were looped over a hook in the garage where I keep the Duesie. I found them in a snarl, straightened them out and put them there. I wondered at the time what anyone did with such thin roping."

"I think tree cutters use it to bring trees down the right direction," Walker said. "I'll keep it."

"Would it hold fingerprints?"

"No, too rough a texture. Let's see where they put your friend."

Henry was on a gurney in a big, white-tiled room with an array of medical instruments on walls and tables.

"Keep out of my way, boys," the burly old doctor said.

"Will he survive?" Walker asked.

"Oh, yeah, he'll live. But he'll have a hell of a headache for a while," the doctor replied.

Henry looked as white as a sheet except for the blood on his face. He was starting to toss about, groaning, and two young men in white clothes had to hold him.

"He got a knock on the side of his head and must have been left on his side where the blood ran into his face," the doctor said, mopping Henry's forehead. "No damage to the face. Where's that nurse with the blood pressure cuff?"

"Right here, sir," a young woman said, rushing in. "The other one wasn't working right."

"It's the damned budget," the doctor groused. "No money to replace important equipment anymore. The damned government. That damned Hoover. We should rename this damned place Hoover Hospital."

He'd wrapped the cuff around Henry's arm and stopped ranting to listen to the stethoscope. "Blood pressure's good. Surprisingly good."

He bent over and pulled Henry's eyelids up, looked at them, flashed a light across. "Pupils okay and reactive."

"Is that good?" Robert asked.

"Very good," the doctor said. "Means there's probably not any brain damage."

"When will we be able to talk to him?" Chief Walker asked.

"Presumably not until he's conscious, you fool. Unless you don't care if he hears you."

Walker swallowed whatever he was about to say while the doctor ripped off one of Henry's shoes and pinched a toe hard. Henry's leg jerked. "Good, good. He's not that far under," the doctor muttered. "Now, you two get out of here and cool your heels. We'll let you know when he wakes up. You boys go get yourselves a drink somewhere and come back in an hour."

They had to be satisfied with that. Even a police chief couldn't overrule a tough old doctor on his own turf.

"There's a place not far from here," Walker said. "Down on the riverfront. Usually open late. The boys down there would love to look over your Duesie," Walker said.

They drove a couple blocks, turned off Route 9 onto a narrow road, descended a long hill, and parked in front of a darkened wooden building perched on a steep slope right next to the Hudson River. The big wooden building climbed three stories up the road.

"It's Myer's Clam Tavern. Best place on the Hudson to eat," Walker said. "Park at the lower level. The two top stories are for the 'working girls.' Only the lowest level has food and booze."

Robert was astonished. Here was a rural speakeasy that called itself a tavern, provided prostitutes and nobody cared. He was used to the sophistication of New York City, but Poughkeepsie appeared to be way ahead in the tolerance game.

Walker, unaware of Robert's thoughts, continued, "The building's been here since 1866 and in the Myers family since 1871."

And have the working girls been here all that time? Robert wondered.

"Don't let the lack of light in the windows fool you," Walker said as they got out of the automobile. He tapped two times at the door on the lower level, waited a moment, tapped twice, waited again and tapped once.

The door opened slightly and someone said, "Jeez! It's the cops!" and tried to slam the door. But Walker already had his foot in the way. There were sounds of mad scrambling from inside.

"Sam, it's me," Walker said.

"Oh." The door opened again. "Jeepers Creepers! Take a look at this car out here, boys."

Roberts and Walker stood aside as a dozen men poured out of the building to examine the Duesie. Then they went inside and sat down at a table. A downtrodden waitress came to the table. "Hiya, Howard. How's tricks?"

"Not too bad. I'm on duty. Just ginger beer for me."

Robert ordered scotch.

The waitress ogled Robert when she brought the drinks back. "You're quite a number. Haven't seen you around before."

"Out-of-towner," Walker said.

"But not far out of town," Robert said and winked at her.

When she'd gone, Walker asked, "You're sure about this rope? It was in your garage?"

"I thought it was familiar when I tried to get it off Henry's hands and I took a quick look at the wall when I pulled the Duesie out of the garage.

The rope that was there is gone. But anybody could have taken it. The garage door barely latches, much less locks. And there were about a million people around all day. Lots of men and boys going down there to take a look at the Duesie."

"I'm curious about his feet not being bound as well as his hands," Walker said. "I'm curious about the whole thing. Why truss him up that way and leave him to possibly die of thirst or exposure when you could bump him off?"

Robert thought for a while. "Maybe whoever did it didn't intend to kill him there. Maybe he meant to take him somewhere else. Maybe it really was a kidnapping attempt and somebody else came along."

"He or she," Walker said.

"Could a woman have done all that? How'd she knock him out to tie him up?"

"I dunno. There's certainly enough dead wood around to bop someone with a big chunk of it. But anybody approaching would make noise."

"Henry wouldn't notice," Robert said. "When he gets a bee in his bonnet, he pays *no* attention to anything else."

"The perfect kind of victim," Walker said with irritation. "I'll have to go back and look at the scene to see if there was a weapon, but it's pretty hopeless. Everybody came running when you yelped and they all stumbled around messing up the ground."

Robert glanced at his watch. "It hasn't been an hour yet, but let's go back and see if he's conscious."

Chapter 22

Henry was awake and furious. And as dumb as a brick. He didn't know where he was or how he got there, nor could he remember what he last did. And he wanted to go home, but couldn't quite recall where home was, which made him even angrier.

"He'll get his memory back," the doctor assured Howard and Robert. "Might take a while. What he needs now is a good ten hours' sleep."

"Are you keeping him here?" Robert asked.

"Long enough to stitch up the cut in his head. We did an X-ray. No harm done to his thick skull. Just a hairline fracture less than an inch long. We should be able to let you have him back around noon tomorrow. Who's paying for this?"

"He will. He's worth millions."

"Am I?" Henry asked.

The doctor looked at Henry. "He sure doesn't look like it."

It was three in the morning before Robert and Howard got back to Grace and Favor. They spoke as they drove back, in a lethargic manner, of the attack on Henry.

"No matter how it happened, what with the ropes and all, I can't figure why it happened to him of all people," Walker said. "He seems about the most harmless person in the whole mess."

"I suppose it was the calling system," Robert said, slowing down and peering ahead. It had become seriously foggy along the river.

"The calling system?"

"Henry hooked up telephone wires to all the bedrooms. That's why nobody saw much of him. He spent most of his time in the servants' basement, threading it along somehow where the old bell pull system was. And putting speakers in the rooms."

"I talked to him before about it, but didn't ask why he was doing it."

Robert shrugged. "Because he's Mad Henry. I suppose the idea had come to him and Grace and Favor struck him as a good place to test it out. It was meant to improve the bell pull system to the basement servants' kitchen and dining room. Not that there have been servants down there for years. He said instead of a guest or resident just ringing the bell and a servant having to go to the second or third floor to find out why, then go back down to the basement or wherever to tend to the matter, Henry thought the person could call down to the servants' hall and say what he or she needed."

"Thereby saving the nonexistent servants trouble?"

"Right."

"And how did it work?"

"Pretty well, though, as I saw, it was useless."

"No, I meant could people really talk back and forth on it or was it a one-way thing? I didn't question him as closely as I should have about how it worked."

"As I understand it, each room had a little speaker box and so did the servants' hall. In the individual rooms they had a choice of listen, talk or off. Controlled by a switch."

"So eavesdropping on someone was possible."

"Not only possible, but I tried it myself," Robert admitted. "Henry set all the switches to 'talk' while everybody else was at dinner. I went down later and listened. All I heard was snoring and some jumbled voices. The reception is very bad. The closer the person is to the thing, the louder and clearer the voice is, but apparently if you get farther away, the voice fades and static takes over. I gave up when Agatha barked in my ear deafeningly."

"I wouldn't tell this to anyone else if I were you," Walker said.

"Why?"

"It's obvious. Somebody else might have figured out the system and feared that Henry had overheard something to their disadvantage."

"That's exactly what I had in mind the night I listened in. But Henry was interested only in whether or not it worked. Not what was being said. He's remarkably single-minded."

"You know that because you know him. Nobody else did. Someone could have regarded him as a very serious threat."

They were silent for the next couple miles. "Okay. It's possible. But there are other possibilities."

"Like what?" Walker asked.

"Anybody might have been up to something

nasty in the woods and feared that Henry had seen them at it," Robert said.

"Aside from the obvious naughtiness of courting couples, what could that have been?"

"I don't know. Disposing of some sort of evidence, maybe? What if the person who murdered Mrs. Ethridge had left something else behind in the room and realized it before Mimi went on her cleaning spree and felt the need to get rid of it?"

"That doesn't make sense," Walker said. "If no one knew this mysterious object had been in her room, what would be the point in disposing of it?"

Robert shrugged. "I don't know. I'm just casting around for other explanations. But I repeat, Henry pays attention to only one thing at a time and wouldn't have even noticed if someone were standing right next to him. But as you say, nobody would know that."

Walker glanced at his watch. "I'll have to be back in Poughkeepsie when he wakes up to hear what he does remember."

Grace and Favor was dark and silent when they returned. Robert showed Walker where the rope had been hung in the garage, and Walker merely nodded wearily and headed for the mansion.

Lily had assigned Walker a room on the third floor since he was determined to stay at Grace and Favor until Mrs. Ethridge's murder was solved. He was so exhausted that he had to stop at each landing and work up the energy to tackle the next. While he paused, he glanced down the hallways. No lights showing anywhere. Maybe everybody would have the good sense to stay where they belonged all night long.

He'd sent one of his deputies to his home with a key to get fresh clothing, a razor and a toothbrush for him and was relieved to see the items laid out on a chair by the window. He undressed and put on his ratty old dressing gown and went down the hall to the gents to brush his teeth. When he came back, he set his alarm for seven-thirty, turned out the light and tried to review everything about the case.

After all the interviews, the observance of the people, the conversations he'd overheard, he should know more than he did. He couldn't keep these people here forever. They were due to leave the next day and he'd have to let them all go their separate ways.

And with that thought, he fell fast asleep.

Mr. Prinney was in his small office at Grace and Favor at eight-thirty when Howard Walker knocked on the door.

"Come in. I've been hoping to talk to you, but didn't want to disturb you. You and Robert must have come home very late."

"Around three," Howard said, all but collapsing in the guest chair.

"I've made some calls to bankers I know to get an introduction to the president of the bank where Mrs. Ethridge lived. The man was willing to cooperate."

"And . . . ?"

"Mrs. Ethridge had a very small income from a family trust. Enough to live on, barely. She made a quarterly deposit of a check from an attorney in Chicago. She had consulted with the banker I spoke with about getting a pension as surviving spouse of a Great War veteran, but there must have been some sort of snarl up because she never deposited a government check. But she made other regular deposits. In cash."

"Blackmail?" Howard asked.

"Possibly. One was for twenty dollars, another for twenty-five dollars and another for thirty dollars. Every month since her husband died. The banker I spoke to had never had occasion to look at her account carefully and was surprised. He knows her very slightly socially, and couldn't explain these regular deposits. Apparently she had no other means of support except the trust. She didn't work in a shop or take in sewing or anything like that. He didn't mention blackmail, of course. But I could tell it was probably on his mind."

"You told him that she had died?"

"Just that she had died. Not *how* she died. Oh, he also gave me the name of the funeral parlor the body should be sent to. I have it here somewhere." He rummaged in a drawer in his desk and produced a scrap of paper.

"She also had a safety deposit box at the bank," Mr. Prinney said, "but you'll have to get the proper authorization to open it. The banker can't do that."

"Did she have a will?"

"There might be one in the box, but as far as he knew she had no attorney. Otherwise she wouldn't have asked his advice about the pension. He suggested two names of attorneys in the town and said she might have dealt with one of them over the pension matter."

"Didn't Miss Brewster give me a New York address for her?" Walker said, checking his notebook. "Yes, here it is."

"Maybe it's her brother's apartment," Mr. Prinney said. "I think Lily told me Mrs. Ethridge arrived in a car with a driver her brother had loaned to her, which was why she arrived early. She might visit him often and use his address."

"Who is her brother?" Walker asked.

"I have no idea," Prinney said. "Somebody Pratt, I presume. If they're full siblings."

"There are going to be a lot of Pratts in New York City. I'll get one of my people find a phone book and try to reach the right one. Didn't Raymond Cameron say something about working in his attorney uncle's office and having seen her name on paperwork?"

"Yes, and I called his uncle as well. He said that some years ago, she had come to him to consult about various run-down properties she owned. They both agreed that the small income didn't justify extensive repairs and she'd be better off selling them as they were and reinvesting the cash. When he'd attended to all the sales, she announced that she was going to use the money for a nice long trip. He was so annoyed with this stupidity that he told her to find another attorney and he hasn't heard from her since then," Mr. Prinney said.

"So we know nothing about her except that she had three unidentifiable sources of income. Maybe blackmail. Maybe just house rentals or something else perfectly legal."

"I'm afraid so. I did my best."

"I know you did, and I'm grateful."

Howard got up from the guest chair and stretched. "I'm going to have breakfast and then go see if Henry's awake yet. I think I'll take Robert along. Henry's more likely to talk freely to him than to me."

Before leaving, Robert and Howard went back to where Henry had been found. As Walker had predicted, there was no evidence of significance at the scene. And if there had been, it had been trampled. There were half a dozen fallen limbs about, any one of which might have been the weapon. None of them showed any noticeable traces of blood and even if they had, Walker said it would prove nothing except that Henry had been hit with it.

"Oh, for a bloody baseball bat with a nice smooth handle with fingerprints," Robert lamented. All they did find was Henry's leather satchel and a strange metal instrument.

Henry was speaking, but it wasn't much help. He had no idea what had happened to him. No memory of being struck down and tied up.

Walker tried to lead him up to it gently. "Start with the last thing you do remember," he said.

Henry screwed up his face, trying to recall. He had a big white bandage wrapped around his head, hair sticking out every which way, and looked idiotic. "I had this gadget to measure the age of trees. I wanted to try out it."

"And did you?"

"I don't know. Did anybody bring it along with me? I'd hate to lose it without knowing whether it works."

"Yes, Robert and I picked it up this morning and left it at Grace and Favor. In the kitchen, I think. A hollow tube with four hooks and a cranking mechanism?"

"Yes, that's it. Was there a core of wood in the tube?"

"I don't think so," Walker said.

"Then I must not have attached it to the tree yet."

"We found a leather satchel, too. Was that yours?"

Henry nodded. The effort made him wince.

"Should there have been anything else in the satchel?" Robert asked. "It was empty when we found it."

"No, the tree coring thing was all I had along, I think."

"How did you pick out which tree to sample?" Walker asked, hoping to encourage Henry's memory.

"I don't remember. But I want to go home."

"We'll take you back to Grace and Favor, Henry," Robert said. "And look after you until your parents can come fetch you. You shouldn't be driving for a while."

"I could drive perfectly well. I learned that long before I got smacked in the head."

"Lily has hidden your keys," Robert improvised. "And you don't want to argue with her, do you?"

Chapter 23

Henry slept most of the way back to Grace and Favor, but woke as the Duesie pulled up to the front door. He got quite a reception. Phoebe had just returned from church and was talking with Lily in the doorway. Mrs. Prinney came out to greet him with offers of a really hearty lunch that would put him right. "We were waiting until you returned to serve it," she said, not adding that they were also waiting for Phoebe to return.

"Poor Henry," Phoebe said, looking at his bandaged head.

"Don't you need to rest a bit?" Lily asked.

Henry wasn't used to this sort of attention and got embarrassed. Mostly when people paid attention to him, it was to laugh. "I *would* like some food," he said modestly.

Luncheon was a few leftovers, cleverly disguised, a huge salad, cold cuts and homemade rye bread. There was a steaming soup tureen full of leeks, potatoes and onions in a cream base. Everyone was hungry and there was little conversation.

But Howard Walker noticed that Henry kept

casting quick glances at Julian West, as though he were perplexed about something.

As West patted his mouth with a napkin and rose from the table, he looked at Walker for a long, angry moment and said, "My train is at two-thirty. I *shall* be leaving here. Should I call for a taxi to the station, or will a ride be provided?"

"We'll see about that," Walker said ambiguously. "Henry, could I have a word with you?"

He led Henry to Mr. Prinney's office, closed the door firmly and said very quietly, "Why did you keep looking at Mr. West during lunch?"

"I remembered something. I saw him in the woods while I was picking out which tree to try the coring machine on."

"Near you?"

"Walking on a path, perhaps twenty feet away. In front of where I was facing."

"What was he doing?"

"Looking around. As if he were searching for something. No, somebody. He wasn't looking down at the ground as you would for a lost object. And a few minutes later, I remember hearing very light footsteps somewhere behind me. I assumed it was Lily Brewster, come to see how the coring gadget worked. I'd run into her shortly before and she'd expressed an interest."

Walker was sitting behind Mr. Prinney's desk, his hands steepled and fingertips to his lips. "I see. Henry, don't mention this to anyone else."

There was a brisk knock on the door and Dr. Polhemus, in his Sunday suit, came in the room. "There you are, young man. I heard about your accident in the woods. Sorry I wasn't still around. I had a maternity case that turned out to be twins,

and was right in the neighborhood. Somebody
should have called me. I could have run right over
and patched you up."

Henry just stared at him.

"So, let's take a look at what they did to you in
Poughkeepsie. Shame you had to go so far. I could
have fixed you up right here."

"Henry, stay here with the doctor," Howard
Walker said. "I need to have a quick word with
Mr. West."

He found that most of the party had moved to
the yellow parlor after lunch. It was a lovely spring
day and the windows and doors were wide open,
letting in light and fresh breezes. Cecil was standing by the outside door, chatting with Lily and
Phoebe about the paths that wound through the
woods and expressing a wish to come back someday and walk them thoroughly.

"Phoebe should be your guide," Lily said. "She
knows her way the best of any of us."

Robert was pouring himself and Raymond a
drink. Rachel and Addie were sitting together on a
sofa having a conversation about hairstyles. Or
rather, Rachel was. Addie was merely listening
with bemusement that anyone could be that interested in the way her hair looked. Mimi and Bud
Carpenter were tidying up the room, cleaning ash-
trays and gathering empty glasses. Apparently the
yellow parlor had been the gathering place most of
the morning as well.

Julian West had taken up his familiar pose by
the fireplace, now cold and screened. He had a
drink in his hand and glared as Walker entered the
room.

Walker said, "I'm afraid you won't be leaving

today, Mr. West. I have some more questions to ask of you."

West drew himself up and, making a dramatic gesture, flung his drink at the fireplace, unaware that it was screened. The glass, almost full, bounced back, splattering him, Rachel and Addie. Rachel jumped up with a yelp.

But West shouted her down.

"I'm sick to death of you people. All of you. I'm leaving here no matter what your bucolic cop says." His voice rose. "I came here, against my will I might add, as an honored guest and have been treated as a criminal."

Bud put down the ashtray he was about to leave the room with and said, "Now, now, Captain West—"

"Shut up, Bud!" West shouted.

Rachel and Addie scooted away from him fearfully as Bud approached.

West was entirely out of control. "I'm a respected person! I write good books that sell well no matter what anyone says. I will not be confined to this great mausoleum of a house any longer, being questioned and prodded by a small-town police chief who wants to make his mark on the world!"

He suddenly turned toward the fireplace and put his hand out to support himself, knocking several ornaments to the floor where they shattered.

Lily and Phoebe were clutching each other in horror at the scene of West going to pieces. Cecil tried to urge them out the door, but they were frozen in place.

Walker, Robert and Bud were all moving slowly toward West.

West turned back to the room. His face was as

white as chalk, the scars more obvious than ever. His face was twisted in agony and he clutched at his left arm with his right, twisting and screaming with pain. As he started to topple forward, Bud and Robert caught him and lowered him to the floor.

The door to the hall burst open and Dr. Polhemus rushed in. "What's happening here!" He saw the other men bending over West and rushed to push them away.

"He's having a heart attack," Polhemus said. "Get back. Don't crowd him. You!" he said, pointing at Raymond, "get my medical bag from Prinney's office. Give the man air. Lift him to the sofa and bring me a light. Then everybody but Walker get out of here."

Stunned, everybody but one did as they were told.

Robert pushed Lily, Cecil and Phoebe through the outside door and followed them onto the lawn. Lily and Phoebe, still arm in arm and trembling violently, sat down on a bench. Robert stood staring back at the doorway. Cecil lowered himself to the grass and sat cross-legged, head down, pale and shaken.

"I'm not leaving the Captain," they heard Bud saying loudly. "It's my duty to be with him."

Polhemus replied, "Just stay out of my way. Where's the idiot with my bag?"

Eventually those not directly involved reassembled silently in the entry hall, waiting, unable to speak or look at one another.

Rachel was weeping from sheer nerves. Lily wanted to slap her silly. But Mimi stepped in and with Raymond's help gently took her upstairs to her room. Cecil asked Robert quietly where the nearest bathroom was, looking downright ill himself.

Phoebe, in a trembling voice, said, "I'm going for a walk," and walked unsteadily out the front door, adding, "I want to pray for him."

Robert and Lily stood staring at each other. Lily finally said, "Where are Mr. and Mrs. Prinney?"

"Mrs. Prinney's in the kitchen, crashing around dishes. Can't you hear her? She knows nothing of this. And Mr. Prinney went to get gas for his car right after lunch."

"Wait here. I'll tell Mrs. Prinney," Lily said.

She was back in a moment with Mrs. Prinney fussing over her. "This is just terrible!" she exclaimed.

There was no way to respond, and no one had to, because just then Dr. Polhemus came out of the yellow parlor at the same time. "I'm sorry," he said. "The man has expired. I did all I could. Walker and West's manservant will take care of the arrangements. The manservant is taking it very badly. I didn't have any sleeping powders along, but he needs to be sedated. I'll go to my office and get some and return. I just need to call about having the body taken away first. There will have to be an autopsy. Sudden death, you know. Even though there's no question it was a heart attack."

Robert took a quick look in the yellow parlor from the doorway. All he could see of West was his feet hanging over the end of the sofa. Walker was sitting on the sofa opposite. Bud Carpenter was standing at the outside door, back to the room, leaning against the jamb. His shoulders were shaking.

Robert quietly closed the door and turned to speak to Lily, but she was gone. The entry hall was empty and silent as a tomb.

Lily had taken Agatha and her dog brush out on the lawn and was sitting watching the river flow past and absentmindedly brushing the dog. She had to do something normal. Something ordinary and boring that had nothing to do with people and their passions.

But her mind was in a whirl—comments she'd heard, impressions she'd had, looks she'd seen exchanged were jostling in her mind. Two deaths. One near-death attack. It couldn't be coincidence. There had to be a pattern. A reason.

And suddenly, one thing stood out. Something Phoebe had said the day before that meant absolutely nothing at the time. And a comment Cecil had made the first night. The two thoughts crashed together with a mental clang.

Lily stood up so suddenly that she startled Agatha, who yelped an objection.

Everything fit. If one thing she didn't know was true. How would she find out? If that one fact was wrong, she had nothing. But if it were right, it would explain everything else.

Cecil! Where was Cecil? He and Dr. Polhemus had the keys to it all.

She came in the house as calmly as possible, though her heart was thumping. Mrs. Prinney was drying the last of the luncheon dishes. "Where's Professor Hoornart?" Lily asked her.

"He came through here looking sick as a dog and

said he was going to his room. Lily, what's wrong? You look feverish."

Lily took off without answering and ran up the steps. She was breathless by the time she reached Cecil's room. He called, "Come in" to her knock.

"That letter you got from the old nanny," Lily said. "Do you have it here? Let me see it."

He looked alarmed by her curt behavior, but took the letter Phoebe had written down from the phone message out of his bedside table drawer and handed it over.

Lily skimmed it quickly. "Yes. That could be it. Cecil, she says at the end that she has a telephone. "You must call her and ask one question. This is what it is. . . ."

Twenty minutes later she had her answer. Only one more thing to find out. Lily paced around at the front door, waiting for Dr. Polhemus to return. When his car came into the drive, she ran to meet it.

"Dr. Polhemus, there is one very important thing you must find out and tell me."

"Yes?"

"Examine Mr. West's body thoroughly before it's taken away. Tell me if he has any other serious scars."

"All in good time, my dear. That will be noted in the autopsy."

"By that time, a murderer may have escaped. You must do it now. By yourself. Must I ask Chief Walker to make this request?"

"Oh, very well."

Lily told him exactly what to look for and followed him to the yellow parlor. Bud Carpenter was now sitting on the sofa across from the body of his dead master. He had his head in his hands.

"Sir, I must make one more examination," Dr. Polhemus said. "Miss Brewster will take you to the kitchen and I'll be through in a moment."

Bud got up like a mechanical toy. Expressionless, he followed Lily. Mrs. Prinney was just washing out a dishcloth and said, "Oh, Mr. Carpenter, I'm so very sorry about Mr. West's death. It must be horrible for you. Let me get you a big glass of warm milk. That's always soothing."

Lily left him there and went in search of Robert and Walker. She found Robert slumped in the visitor chair in Mr. Prinney's office while Walker spoke on the telephone to the local funeral home.

"Lily, you're pale as a ghost," Robert said, getting up and forcing her into the comfortable chair. Walker hung up the phone. Lily perched at the front of the chair like a fledgling bird about to take a first, terrifying flight.

"I think I know how this all happened. I just don't know quite where to start."

"Start anywhere," Walker said, looking at her intently.

"Well, I told Phoebe about what Henry had heard on the calling system, and she said, 'What kind of appendix?' I told her the kind in the back of a book with extra information."

"Right," Walker said.

"No, wrong. Cecil spoke with West in his room about the book appendix. But the conversation I think Henry overheard was between West and Lorna Ethridge in her room about his appendix. West's, I mean."

Walker and Robert exchanged looks that clearly meant: Has she gone off her rocker?

Lily knew what they were thinking and wondered if they might be right.

"The dead man on the sofa isn't Julian West," she said.

Chapter 24

Walker checked Lily's story with Cecil and Dr. Polhemus, who confirmed what they'd both learned. Then he asked everyone to come to the yellow parlor. Mr. Prinney had come home from his errand and Robert filled him in on what had happened during his absence.

"All that? I was only gone for half an hour."

Robert had to conceal a smile. He'd never known Mr. Prinney to be funny, even inadvertently.

The guests and residents, plus Dr. Polhemus, assembled once again in the yellow parlor. Lily was considering closing it up when this was over. At the moment, she couldn't imagine ever wanting to come back in this room, lovely and comfortable as it was.

Only Rachel had flatly refused to be present. "We don't need her," Walker said. "Let her stay in her room."

He took Julian West's place in front of the fireplace. It was four o'clock and the sky had clouded over so the doors had been shut and the lights turned on. Bud Carpenter was again sitting on the sofa where West had died. Robert sat beside him.

Raymond stood behind the sofa. Dr. Polhemus and Mr. Prinney were on the opposite sofa. The women were around the sides of the room.

Bud still looked like he'd been pole-axed, though he'd absolutely refused to take the sleeping powders that Dr. Polhemus had offered him.

Walker cleared his throat and glanced at Lily. She nodded.

"Mr. Carpenter, we're all sorry for your loss."

Bud shrugged, looking down at his hands folded in his lap.

"But you didn't lose Julian West today, did you?" Walker went on. "You lost him in the Great War, in the Argonne Forest. The man's body that was taken away was that of his cousin, John West. Isn't that true?"

Bud looked up at Walker with resigned hatred. "What if it is?"

"You admit it?"

"I admit nothing."

"Then I will tell you. Julian West, who wrote such fine novels, was the mentor of his cousin. It was Julian who died in the fire in the trenches and John who survived and kept writing war novels."

"What makes you think that?" Bud said lethargically.

"Because Professor Hoornart is in touch with the woman who was Julian West's governess or nanny when he was a child. She's told us that when he was a small child, he had his appendix removed. The surgeon didn't sew up the incision properly and the stitches burst. It had to be resewn and got another external infection. He was left with a terrible scar. The man who died had no such scar. Not even a hint of one. Dr. Polhemus has confirmed this."

Bud sat back slightly. His face was as expressionless as when he was waiting table at the meals.

"You agreed with the charade. That John West would replace his cousin. They must have looked quite a lot alike. The nanny confirms this was true when they were children, at least. And the scars on John West's face could account for any difference in the supposed Julian West's appearance when he returned from the war."

"It was Captain Julian's idea," Bud said tonelessly. "Before he died. He said he wanted his name to go on and only his cousin John could make that happen."

A great silence fell over the room and Walker let it go on as long as he could stand. "But Lorna Pratt Ethridge had been his lover as a young woman. That story was probably the only one of herself that was true. She knew the scar. And when she invited herself to Julian's room after Professor Hoornart had left, and made love to him here, she knew it wasn't the same man. Maybe she'd already guessed and came to his room to prove it to herself. She was a blackmailer, you know."

"She was a bitch," Bud said under his breath.

"You were in the next room. You heard them."

Bud finally looked up again. He was still expressionless as he said flatly, "She told him she had money problems. That he would either marry her and leave his fortune to her in his will, or she would reveal that he was an imposter."

"So you protected him from her threats."

"It was my job to," Bud said blandly, as if anyone in his right senses could understand. "When

Mr. John West and I were taking Mr. Julian West back from the front, he said John was to take his place. And he made me swear I would remain as true to his cousin as I had been to him."

Walker wasn't as interested in the distant past as in the recent. "You followed Mrs. Ethridge to her room," Walker said just as coolly. "And killed her, and left West's tie tack on the floor so that he would be accused, and you could absolutely refute the charge, thus protecting him from further suspicion. And it almost worked. You fooled me," he admitted. "You were very good at your 'job,' weren't you?"

"Yes, I was," Bud said, straightening his back a bit. "Those two men were my life. My way out of poverty and ignorance. I owed them."

"And the manuscript? You stole that, too."

"I had to. I heard that man"—he pointed to Cecil, who quailed slightly—"I heard him say that the books were written before and after the Great War by a different man. I couldn't have him saying that in a book. I didn't like killing Lorna Pratt, you know. And I didn't want to kill again. But I've seen, man and boy, how hard it is to write a book, and I know if it were lost, no writer would have the heart to start over on the same book."

At this, Lily couldn't stop herself from speaking. "You didn't hear what else Professor Hoornart said because you were called away. He said it was the Great War that changed Julian West the researcher of facts into Julian West the man who had actually lived them. He didn't mean it literally. Although he was right, but didn't know it."

"It doesn't matter, miss. Nothing matters anymore. I did my job. I protected the two men who had saved my life and made me worthwhile."

A chill seemed to fall over everyone in the room at this remorselessly honest remark.

Lily said, almost the second she was realizing it, "I saw you standing near the edge of the woods during the morning yesterday. I thought you looked fatter than usual. You had the manuscript under your shirt, didn't you?"

Bud didn't even turn to look at her. "I was going to throw it in the river with that rope from the garage tied around it. But there was no way to do that without being seen, I realized, and it might have floated. So I went into the woods, thinking to bury it. Then I ran into that loony little man with the satchel. I couldn't let him see me. So I hit him."

His voice and manner were so cool, so seemingly reasonable, that Lily felt sick. "You didn't know, for all your eavesdropping, that Henry had heard the conversation between Mrs. Ethridge and Mr. West about the appendix?"

"Why, no, miss. If I'd known that I'd have killed him outright." He thought for a moment and went on, "I was going to drag him farther away from the paths, deeper into the woods, and then I heard Mr. West walking nearby. I knew from his tread. He had a way of putting his right foot down just a little harder than his left. I don't think any of you noticed that, did you?"

He glanced around the room calmly, as if he were talking about nothing more serious than the weather. "I didn't want Mr. West to know what I'd done for him. It wouldn't be seemly. And with his bad temper, it wouldn't be safe for me. He was likely to fly off the handle someday and say something he shouldn't. So I left the little man and buried the manuscript deeper in the woods and decided not to go back to him. No point in him dying, too. He didn't know anything. And I knew he'd be found. I'd have found him myself in another hour if someone else didn't."

Walker said, "You don't appear to have any guilt about any of this."

"But I do," Bud said. "I was doing my job. Taking care of Captain West, but I hadn't known that the Captain saw me in the woods with the little man. That's why he was so upset that he had a heart attack. It's my fault he died."

He got up slowly, like an old man. "And now I have two more jobs. I must put his things in order. And my own, so you can take me to jail. I'll probably be executed. It doesn't matter. I have no life anymore. And if not, I'll make a good prisoner. I'm very well organized, you know."

The rest of the people in the room were too stunned by this statement to react.

Walker finally cleared his throat. "Very well. We'll have to get your statement in writing and signed. Robert, will you call the county sheriff to pick him up? Dr. Polhemus, I'd like you to accompany me and Mr. Carpenter upstairs."

The three of them walked up the steps very formally, almost like a military honor guard with Bud Carpenter in the middle. Walker himself could hardly believe how calm Carpenter was. And how calm he himself was.

They entered the larger room and Bud set about gathering John West's clothing and belongings. He folded the clothes neatly and efficiently. Put the extra pair of shoes into flannel shoe bags in order not to soil the rest of the clothing.

Walker watched, amazed. The clothing would probably go to some charity or another. What was the point in being so orderly? But Bud Carpenter had probably always been an obsessively orderly man. Let him do this one last thing for West.

When Bud was almost done and the suitcase was nearly full, he started toward the door to the rest of the suite. Walker had been sitting down on a chair. He rose and said, "Where are you going?"

"To get Mr. West's shaving things," as if it were obvious they couldn't be left behind. It would be a dereliction of his duty.

Walker started to follow, but turned when Dr. Polhemus said, "The man is utterly insane."

Walker was about to respond when the gunshot rang out.

Chapter 25

By Sunday night, all the guests were gone except Cecil, who had found his dirty but readable manuscript buried behind the garage. The Prinneys, the Brewsters, Phoebe, Mimi, Cecil and Jack Summer were sitting around the huge dining room table all at one end so they didn't have to shout at one another.

Jack Summer was angry. "You could have called me when you figured it out. I could have been here for a real scoop."

"I'm sorry. I just didn't think about scoops. I was thinking about a murderer who was on the verge of getting away with it," Lily said, for the third time.

Jack had another grievance. "And Chief Walker should have known that a man like that would carry his service revolver with him everywhere."

Cecil said, "Maybe he did. Maybe he wanted to spare Bud Carpenter an execution at the hands of others or an empty lifetime as a prisoner. You weren't here, young man. You didn't see what an utterly empty shell Carpenter had become without Julian—or rather John—West. He'd murdered for

West and he believed he'd caused West's death. If Walker guessed at the presence of a revolver, I think it was a kind act to pretend he didn't. Carpenter would have killed himself sooner or later and this was the fastest, easiest way."

Jack subsided somewhat. "Maybe so."

"What I don't understand yet," Mrs. Prinney said, "is how that peculiar little Henry could have mistaken Mrs. Ethridge's voice for Professor Hoornart's when he was fooling around with listening to different rooms."

"Oh, I can," Robert said. "First, Henry really wasn't interested in who was talking beyond figuring out which room's speaker was working properly. And secondly, Lorna Ethridge had a very deep, sexy voice that could have sounded like a man's."

"I suppose she did, come to think of it," Mrs. Prinney allowed.

Mr. Prinney grumbled, "I went to a lot of trouble investigating her finances and came to the conclusion that she was a blackmailer. I still believe she was, but I'll never know now. I had such high hopes that blackmail was the motive."

"You're right," Robert said. "We won't know. But at least three people will be very grateful to hear that she's dead and probably take their husbands or wives out to a very nice dinner with the money they'll be saving next month."

"Robert, that's very flip," Lily said disapprovingly.

"I agree with Robert," Cecil said. "The woman messed up nearly every life she touched. Including yours. She's no loss to humanity. But how will you ever manage to have guests again in this house when they hear one guest was murdered and the guest of honor dropped dead of a heart attack?"

"Most people love disasters," Robert said. "That's why they flock to the scenes of accidents. We'll do fine. I can hardly wait to get the word out."

"I've got my article almost done for the paper," Jack Summer said. "I'm sure some other papers, especially the New York City ones, will pick it up. Julian West, who turned out to be John West, was a famous man and I wouldn't mind a bit seeing my byline in a City paper."

"And I'll get a book out of it that will sell like mad," Cecil added. "All the details, firsthand, that can't go into a newspaper article. I'm afraid I have to admit that Bud Carpenter did me a great favor."

"Speaking of book sales," Lily said, "what did West mean when he was ranting and said that his books sold well no matter what anyone said?"

Cecil gazed at her with a look almost of pity. "I guess you have no reason to watch the publishing world as closely as I do. His books weren't selling as well as they used to."

"But nothing is selling as well as it used to. We're in a Depression," Lily said.

"We are, but entertainment—books, movies, plays—have become more valued than ever. People want and need distractions from the daily grind."

Lily thought about the Hollywood property Uncle Horatio owned, which was still paying off its leases handsomely, and of the town movie house which was the only truly profitable business in town. "I guess you're right."

"Word in the City, in publishing circles anyway,

was that Julian West, or the man everybody thought was Julian West, was going to have to 'go on the road' like so many other successful writers do to keep on even having his books accepted."

"The last mystery is solved," Robert said. "Remember how suspicious I was, Lily, when he accepted the invitation?"

"Oh, yes. You harped on it plenty."

Cecil got up from the table. "If I'm to get the last train, I better get going."

"You're welcome to stay tonight," Lily said, thinking that he'd already eaten an extra meal and it wouldn't hurt her precious budget much to let him stay one more night.

"Thank you, but no. I want to be at my desk first thing in the morning, getting this book together while West's death is still in people's memory. But I'll be back someday soon, if Miss Twinkle is willing to loan me her maps again and maybe guide me on nature walks."

Miss Twinkle blushed furiously. "Of course."

Mr. Prinney offered to drive Cecil to the train station and as Lily and Robert stood on the porch, waving them off, Lily said, "Something good came of this."

"You mean we made a profit?" Robert asked.

"We made a profit, solved a murder—and helped along a budding romance."

"Lily," Robert said. "You're a sap."

We hope you have enjoyed this Avon Twilight mystery. Mysteries fascinate and intrigue with the worlds they create. And what better way to capture your interest than this glimpse into the world of a select group of Avon Twilight authors.

Tamar Myers reveals the deadly side of the antique business. The bed-and-breakfast industry becomes lethal in the hands of Mary Daheim. A walk along San Antonio's famed River Walk with Carolyn Hart reveals a fascinating and mysterious place. Nevada Barr encounters danger on Ellis Island. Deborah Woodworth's Sister Rose Callahan discovers something sinister is afoot in her Kentucky Shaker village. Jill Churchill steps back in time to the 1930s along the Hudson River and creates a weekend of intrigue. And Anne George's Southern Sisters find that making money is a motive for murder.

So turn the page for a sneak peek into worlds filled with mystery and murder. And if you like what you read, head to your nearest bookstore. It's the only way to figure out whodunnit . . .

December

Abigail Timberlake, the heroine of Tamar Myers' delightful Den of Antiquity series, is smart, quirky, and strong-minded. She has to be—running your own antique business is a struggle, even on the cultured streets of Charlotte, North Carolina, and her mean-spirited divorce lawyer of an ex-husband's caused her a lot of trouble over the years. She also has a "delicate" relationship with her proper Southern mama.

The difficulties in Abby's personal life are nothing, though, to the trouble that erupts when she buys a "faux" Van Gogh at auction ...

ESTATE OF MIND

by Tamar Myers

You already know that my name is Abigail Timberlake, but you might not know that I was married to a beast of a man for just over twenty years. Buford Timberlake—or Timbersnake, as I call him—is one of Charlotte, North Carolina's most prominent divorce lawyers. Therefore, he knew exactly what he was doing when he traded me in for his secretary. Of course, Tweetie Bird is half my age—

although parts of her are even much younger than that. The woman is 20 percent silicone, for crying out loud, although admittedly it balances rather nicely with the 20 percent that was sucked away from her hips.

In retrospect, however, there are worse things than having your husband dump you for a man-made woman. It hurt like the dickens at the time, but it would have hurt even more had he traded me in for a brainier model. I can buy most of what Tweetie has (her height excepted), but she will forever be afraid to flush the toilet lest she drown the Ty-D-Bol man.

And as for Buford, he got what he deserved. Our daughter, Susan, was nineteen at the time and in college, but our son, Charlie, was seventeen, and a high school junior. In the penultimate miscarriage of justice, Buford got custody of Charlie, our house, and even the dog Scruffles. I must point out that Buford got custody of our friends as well. Sure, they didn't legally belong to him, but where would you rather stake your loyalty? To a good old boy with more connections than the White House switchboard, or to a housewife whose biggest ac-complishment, besides giving birth, was a pie crust that didn't shatter when you touched it with your fork? But like I said, Buford got what he deserved and today—it actually pains me to say this—nei-ther of our children will speak to their father.

Now I own a four bedroom, three bath home not far from my shop. My antique shop is the Den of Antiquity. I paid for this house, mind you—not one farthing came from Buford. At any rate, I share this peaceful, if somewhat lonely, abode with a very hairy male who is young enough to be my son.

When I got home from the auction, I was in need of a little comfort, so I fixed myself a cup of tea with milk and sugar—never mind that it was summer—and curled up on the white cotton couch in the den. My other hand held a copy of Anne Grant's *Smoke Screen*, a mystery novel set in Charlotte and surrounding environs. I hadn't finished more than a page of this exciting read when my roommate rudely pushed it aside and climbed into my lap.

"Dmitri," I said, stroking his large orange head, "that 'Starry Night' painting is so ugly, if Van Gogh saw it, he'd cut off his other ear."

Some folks think that just because I'm in business for myself, I can set my own hours. That's true as long as I keep my shop open forty hours a week during prime business hours and spend another eight or ten hours attending sales. Not to mention the hours spent cleaning and organizing any subsequent purchases. I know what they mean, though. If I'm late to the shop, I may lose a valued customer, but I won't lose my job—at least not in one fell swoop.

I didn't think I'd ever get to sleep Wednesday night, and I didn't. It was well into the wee hours of Thursday morning when I stopped counting green thistles and drifted off. When my alarm beeped, I managed to turn it off in my sleep. Either that or in my excitement, I had forgotten to set it. At any rate, the telephone woke me up at 9:30, a half hour later than the time I usually open my shop.

"*Muoyo webe*," Mama said cheerily.

"What?" I pushed Dmitri off my chest and sat up.

"Life to you, Abby. That's how they say 'good morning' in Tshiluba."

I glanced at the clock. "Oh, shoot! Mama, I've got to run."

"I know, dear. I tried the shop first and got the machine. Abby, you really should consider getting a professional to record your message. Someone who sounds . . . well, more cultured."

"Like Rob?" I remembered the painting. "Mama, sorry, but I really can't talk now."

"Fine," Mama said, her cheeriness deserting her. "I guess, like they say, bad news can wait."

I sighed. Mama baits her hooks with an expertise to be envied by the best fly fishermen.

"Sock it to me, Mama. But make it quick."

"Are you sitting down, Abby?"

"Mama, I'm still in bed!"

"Abby, I'm afraid I have some horrible news to tell you about one of your former boyfriends."

"Greg?" I managed to gasp after a few seconds. "Did something happen to Greg?"

"No, dear, it's Gilbert Sweeny. He's dead."

I wanted to reach through the phone line and shake Mama until her pearls rattled. "Gilbert Sweeny was never my boyfriend!"

From nationally-bestselling author Mary Daheim, who creates a world inside a Seattle bed-and-breakfast that is impossible to resist, comes Creeps Suzette, *the newest addition to this delightful series . . .*

Judith McMonigle Flynn, the consummate hostess of Hillside Manor, fairly flies out the door in the dead of winter when her cousin Renie requests her company. As long as Judith's ornery mother, her ferocious feline, and her newly retired husband aren't joining them, Judith couldn't care less where they're going. That is until they arrive at the spooky vine-covered mansion, Creepers, in which an elderly woman lives in fear that someone is trying to kill her. And it's up to the cousins to determine which dark, drafty corner houses a cold-blooded killer before a permanent hush falls over them all . . .

CREEPS SUZETTE

by Mary Daheim

"As you wish, ma'am," said Kenyon, and creaked out of the parlor.

"Food," Renie sighed. "I'm glad I'm back."

"With a vengeance," Judith murmured. "You know," she went on, "when I saw those stuffed animal heads in the game room, I had to wonder if Kenneth wasn't reacting to them. His grandfather or great-grandfather must have hunted. Maybe he grew up feeling sorry for the lions and tigers and bears, oh, my!"

"I could eat a bear," Renie said.

Climbing the tower staircase, the cousins could feel the wind. "Not well-insulated in this part of the house," Judith noted as they entered Kenneth's room.

"It's a tower," Renie said. "What would you expect?"

Judith really hadn't expected to see Roscoe the raccoon, but there he was, standing on his hind legs in a commodious cage. The bandit eyes gazed soulfully at the cousins.

"Hey," Renie said, kneeling down, "from the looks of that food dish, you've eaten more than we have this evening. You'll have to wait for dessert."

Judith, meanwhile, was studying the small fireplace, peeking into drawers, looking under the bed. "Nothing," she said, opening the door to the nursery. "Just the kind of things you'd expect Kenneth to keep on hand for his frequent visits to Creepers."

Renie said good-bye to Roscoe and followed Judith into the nursery. "How long," Renie mused, "do you suppose it's been since any kids played in here?"

Judith calculated. "Fifteen years, maybe more?"

"Do you think they're keeping it for grandchildren?" Renie asked in a wistful tone.

Judith gave her cousin a sympathetic glance. So

far, none of the three grown Jones offspring had acquired mates or produced children. "That's possible," Judith said. "You shouldn't give up hope, especially these days when kids marry so late."

Renie didn't respond. Instead, she contemplated the train set. "This is the same vintage as the one I had. It's a Marx, like mine. I don't think they make them any more."

"Some of these dolls are much older," Judith said. "They're porcelain and bisque. These toys run the gamut. "From hand-carved wooden soldiers to plastic Barbies. And look at this dollhouse. The furniture is all the same style as many of the pieces in this house."

"Hey," Renie said, joining Judith at the shelf where the dollhouse was displayed, "this looks like a cutaway replica of Creepers itself. There's even a tower room on this one side and it's..." Renie blanched and let out a little gasp.

"What's wrong, coz? Are you okay?" Judith asked in alarm.

A gust of wind blew the door to the nursery shut, making both cousins jump. "Yeah, right, I'm just fine," Renie said in a startled voice. "But look at this. How creepy can Creepers get?"

Judith followed Renie's finger. In the top floor of the half-version of the tower was a bed, a chair, a table, and a tiny doll in a long dark dress. The doll was lying facedown on the floor in what looked like a pool of blood.

The lights in the nursery went out.

Carolyn Hart is the multiple Agatha, Anthony, and Macavity Award-winning author of the "Death on Demand" series as well as the highly praised Henrie O series. In Death on the River Walk, sixtysomething retired journalist Henrietta O'Dwyer Collins must turn her carefully-honed sleuthing skills to a truly perplexing crime that's taken place at the luxurious gift shop Tesoros on the fabled River Walk of San Antonio, Texas. See why the Los Angeles Times said, "If I were teaching a course on how to write a mystery, I would make Carolyn Hart required reading . . .

DEATH ON THE RIVER WALK

by Carolyn Hart

Sirens squalled. When the police arrived, this area would be closed to all of us. Us. Funny. Was I aligning myself with the Garza clan? Not exactly, though I was charmed by Maria Elena, and I liked—or wanted to like—her grandson Rick. But I wasn't kidding myself that the death of the blond man wouldn't cause trouble for Iris. Whatever she'd found in the wardrobe, it had to be connected to this murder. And I wanted a look inside Tescros before Rick had a chance to grab Iris's backpack should it be there. That was why I'd told Rick to make the call to the police from La Mariposa.

The central light was on. That was the golden pool that spread through the open door. The small recessed spots above the limestone display islands were dark, so the rest of the store was dim and shadowy.

I followed alongside the path revealed by Manuel's mop. It was beginning to dry at the farther reach, but there was still enough moisture to tell the story I was sure the police would understand. The body had been moved along this path, leaving a trail of bloodstains. That's what Manuel had mopped up.

The sirens were louder, nearer.

The trail ended in the middle of the store near an island with a charming display of pottery banks—a lion, a bull, a big-cheeked balding man, a donkey, a rounded head with bright red cheeks. Arranged in a semicircle, each was equidistant from its neighbor. One was missing.

I used my pocket flashlight, snaked the beam high and low. I didn't find the missing bank. Or Iris's backpack.

The sirens choked in mid-wail.

I hurried, moving back and forth across the store, swinging the beam of my flashlight. No pottery bank, no backpack. Nothing else appeared out of order or disturbed in any way. The only oddity was the rapidly drying area of freshly mopped floor, a three-foot swath leading from the paperweight-display island to the front door.

I reached the front entrance and stepped outside.

In trying to stay clear of the mopped area, I almost stumbled into the pail and mop. I leaned down, wrinkled my nose against the sour smell of ammonia, and pointed the flashlight beam into the faintly discolored water, no longer foamy with suds. The water's brownish tinge didn't obscure the round pink snout of a pottery pig bank.

Swift, heavy footsteps sounded on the steps leading down from La Mariposa. I moved quickly to stand by the bench. Iris looked with wide and frightened eyes at the policemen following Rick and his Uncle Frank into the brightness spilling out from Tesoros. I supposed Rick had wakened his uncle to tell him of the murder.

Iris reached out, grabbed my hand. Rick stopped a few feet from the body, pointed at it, then at the open door. Frank Garza peered around the shoulder of a short policeman with sandy hair and thick glasses. Rick was pale and strained. He spoke in short, jerky sentences to a burly policeman with ink-black hair, an expressionless face, and one capable hand resting on the butt of his pistol. Frank patted his hair, disarranged from sleep, stuffed his misbuttoned shirt into his trousers.

When Rick stopped, the policeman turned and looked toward the bench. Iris's fingers tightened on mine, but I knew the policeman wasn't looking at us. He was looking at Manuel, sitting quietly with his usual excellent posture, back straight, feet apart, hands loose in his lap.

Manuel slowly realized that everyone was looking at him. He blinked, looked at us eagerly, slowly lifted his hands, and began to clap.

March

*Nevada Barr's brilliant series featuring Park
Ranger Anna Pigeon takes this remarkable heroine
to the scene of heinous crimes at the feet of a national shrine—the Statue of Liberty. While bunk-
ing with friends on Liberty Island, Anna finds
solitude in the majestically decayed remains of hos-
pitals, medical wards, and staff quarters of Ellis
Island. When a tumble through a crumbling staircase temporarily halts her ramblings, Anna is willing to write off the episode as an accident. But then
a young girl falls—or is pushed—to her death
while exploring the Statue of Liberty, and it's up
to Anna to uncover the deadly secrets of Lady Liberty's treasured island.*

LIBERTY FALLING

by Nevada Barr

Held aloft by the fingers of her right hand, Anna
dangled over the ruined stairwell. Between dust
and night there was no way of knowing what lay
beneath. Soon either her fingers would uncurl from
the rail or the rail would pull out from the wall.
Faint protests of aging screws in softening plaster
foretold the collapse. No superhuman feats of

strength struck Anna as doable. What fragment of energy remained in her arm was fast burning away on the pain. With a kick and a twist, she managed to grab hold of the rail with her other hand as well. Much of the pressure was taken off her shoulder, but she was left face to the wall. There was the vague possibility that she could scoot one hand width at a time up the railing, then swing her legs onto what might or might not be stable footing at the top of the stairs. Two shuffles nixed that plan. Old stairwells didn't fall away all in a heap like guillotined heads. Between her and the upper floor were the ragged remains, shards of wood and rusted metal. In the black dark she envisioned the route upward with the same jaundice a hay bale might view a pitchfork.

What the hell, she thought. *How far can it be?* And she let go.

With no visual reference, the fall, though in reality not more than five or six feet, jarred every bone in her body. Unaided by eyes and brain, her legs had no way of compensating. Knees buckled on impact and her chin smacked into them as her forehead met some immovable object. The good news was, the whole thing was over in the blink of a blind eye and she didn't think she'd sustained any lasting damage.

Wisdom dictated she lie still, take stock of her body and surroundings, but this decaying dark was so filthy she couldn't bear the thought of it. Stink rose from the litter: pigeon shit, damp and rot. Though she'd seen none, it was easy to imagine spiders of evil temperament and immoderate size. Easing up on feet and hands, she picked her way over rubble she could not see, heading for the faint smudge of gray that would lead her to the out-of-doors.

Free of the damage she'd wreaked, Anna quickly found her way out of the tangle of inner passages and escaped Island III through the back door of the ward. The sun had set. The world was bathed in gentle peach-colored light. A breeze, damp but cooling with the coming night, blew off the water. Sucking it in, she coughed another colony of spores from her lungs. With safety, the delayed reaction hit. Wobbly, she sat down on the steps and put her head between her knees.

Because she'd been messing around where she probably shouldn't have been in the first place, she'd been instrumental in the destruction of an irreplaceable historic structure. Sitting on the stoop, smeared with dirt and reeking of bygone pigeons, she contemplated whether to report the disaster or just slink away and let the monument's curators write it off to natural causes. She was within a heartbeat of deciding to do the honorable thing when the decision was taken from her.

The sound of boots on hard-packed earth followed by a voice saying: "Patsy thought it might be you," brought her head up. A lovely young man, resplendent in the uniform of the Park Police, was walking down the row of buildings toward her.

"Why?" Anna asked stupidly.

"One of the boat captains radioed that somebody was over here." The policeman sat down next to her. He was no more than twenty-two or -three, fit and handsome and oozing boyish charm. "Have you been crawling around or what?"

Anna took a look at herself. Her khaki shorts

were streaked with black, her red tank top un-
tucked and smeared with vile-smelling mixtures. A
gash ran along her thigh from the hem of her shorts
to her kneecap. It was bleeding, but not profusely.
Given the amount of rust and offal in this adven-
ture, she would have to clean it thoroughly and it
wouldn't hurt to check when she'd last had a tet-
anus shot.

"Sort of," she said, and told him about the stairs.
"Should we check it out? Surely we'll have to make
a report. You'll have to write a report," she
amended. "I'm just a hapless tourist."

The policeman looked over his shoulder. The
doorway behind them was cloaked in early night.
"Maybe in the morning," he said, and Anna could
have sworn he was afraid. There was something in
this strong man's voice that told her, were it a hundred years earlier, he would have made a sign
against the evil eye.

April

Sister Rose Callahan, eldress of the Depression-era community of Believers at the Kentucky Shaker village of North Homage, knows that evil does not merely exist in the Bible. Sometimes it comes very close to home indeed.

"A complete and very charming portrait
of a world, its ways, and the
beliefs of its people, and an
excellent mystery to draw you along."
ANNE PERRY

In the next pages, Sister Rose confronts danger in the form of an old religious cult seeking new members among the peaceful Shakers.

A SIMPLE SHAKER MURDER

by Deborah Woodworth

At first, Rose saw nothing alarming, only rows of strictly pruned apple trees, now barren of fruit and most of their leaves. The group ran through the apple trees and into the more neglected east side of the orchard, where the remains of touchier fruit trees lived out their years with little human attention. The pounding feet ahead of her stopped, and panting bodies piled behind one another, still trying to keep some semblance of separation between the brethren and the sisters.

The now-silent onlookers stared at an aged plum tree. From a sturdy branch hung the limp figure of a man, his feet dangling above the ground. His eyes were closed and his head slumped forward, almost hiding the rope that gouged into his neck. The man wore loose clothes that were neither Shaker nor of the world, and Rose sensed he was gone even before Josie reached for his wrist and shook her head.

Two brethren moved forward to cut the man down.

"Nay, don't, not yet," Rose said, hurrying forward.

Josie's eyebrows shot up. "Surely you don't think this is anything but the tragedy of a man choosing to end his own life?" She nodded past the man's torso to a delicate chair laying on its side in the grass. It was a Shaker design, not meant for such rough treatment. Dirt scuffed the woven red-and-white tape of the seat. Scratches marred the smooth slats that formed its ladder back.

"What's going on here? Has Mother Ann appeared and declared today a holiday from labor?" The powerful voice snapped startled heads backwards, to where Elder Wilhelm emerged from the trees, stern jaw set for disapproval.

No one answered. Everyone watched Wilhelm's ruddy face blanche as he came in view of the dead man.

"Dear God," he whispered. "Is he . . . ?"

"Yea," said Josie.

"Then cut him down instantly," Wilhelm said. His voice had regained its authority, but he ran a shaking hand through his thick white hair.

Eyes turned to Rose. "I believe we should leave him for now, Wilhelm," she said. A flush spread across Wilhelm's cheeks, and Rose knew she was in for a public tongue thrashing, so she explained quickly. "Though all the signs point to suicide, still it is a sudden and brutal death, and I believe we should alert the Sheriff. He'll want things left just as we found them."

"Sheriff Brock . . ." Wilhelm said with a snort of derision. "He will relish the opportunity to find us culpable."

"Please, for the sake of pity, cut him down." A man stepped forward, hat in hand in the presence of death. His thinning blond hair lifted in the wind. His peculiar loose work clothes seemed too generous for his slight body. "I'm Gilbert Owen Griffiths," he said, nodding to Rose. "And this is my compatriot, Earl Weston," he added, indicating a broad-shouldered, dark-haired young man. "I am privileged to be guiding a little group of folks who are hoping to rekindle the flame of the great social reformer, Robert Owen. That poor unfortunate man," he said, with a glance at the dead man, "was Hugh—Hugh Griffiths—and he was one of us. We don't mind having the Sheriff come take a look, but we are all like a family, and it is far too painful for us to leave poor Hugh hanging."

"It's an outrage, leaving him there like that," Earl said. "What if Celia should come along?"

"Celia is poor Hugh's wife," Gilbert explained. "I'll have to break the news to her soon. I beg of you, cut him down and cover him before she shows up."

Wilhelm assented with a curt nod. "I will inform the Sheriff," he said as several brethren cut the man down and lay him on the ground. The morbid fascination had worn off, and most of the crowd was backing away.

There was nothing to do but wait. Rose gathered up the sisters and New-Owenite women who had not already made their escape. Leaving Andrew to watch over the ghastly scene until the Sheriff arrived, she sent the women on ahead to breakfast, for which she herself had no appetite. The men followed behind.

On impulse Rose glanced back to see Andrew's tall figure hunched against a tree near the body. He watched the crowd's departure with a forlorn expression. As she raised her arm to send him an encouraging wave, a move distracted her. She squinted through the tangle of unpruned branches behind Andrew to locate the source. *Probably just a squirrel*, she thought, but her eyes kept searching nonetheless. There it was again—a flash of brown almost indistinguishable from tree bark. Several rows of trees back from where Andrew stood, something was moving among the branches of an old pear tree—something much bigger than a squirrel.

May

Once upon a time Lily and Robert were the pam-
pered offspring of a rich New York family. But the
crash of '29 left them virtually penniless until a
distant relative offered them a Grace and Favor
house on the Hudson.

The catch is they must live at this house for ten
years and not return to their beloved Manhattan.
In In the Still of the Night Lily and Robert invite
paying guests from the city to stay with them for
a cultural weekend. But then something goes
wildly askew.

IN THE STILL OF THE NIGHT

by Jill Churchill

"I realized that Mrs. Ethridge wasn't at breakfast
and she hasn't come to lunch either. I kept an eye
out for her so I could nip in and tidy her room
while she was out and about and she hasn't been."

"She's not in the dining room?" Lily said. "No,
I guess not. There were two empty chairs."

"She might be sick, miss."

"Have you knocked on her door?"

"A couple times, miss."

"I'll go see what's become of her," Lily said.

Robert, who had been ringing up the operator, hung up the phone. "I think it would be better for me to check on her."

"But Robert . . ." Lily saw his serious expression and paused. "Very well. But I'll come with you."

They went up to the second floor and Robert tapped lightly on the door. "Mrs. Ethridge? Are you all right?" When there was no response, he tapped more firmly and repeated himself loudly.

They stood there, brother and sister, remembering another incident last fall, and staring at each other. "I'll look. You stay out here," Robert said.

He opened the door and almost immediately closed it in Lily's face. She heard the snick of the inside lock. There was complete silence for a long moment, then Robert unlocked and re-opened the door. "Lily, she's dead."

Lily gasped. "Are you sure?"

"Quite sure."

"Oh, why did she have to die *here*?" Lily said, then caught herself. "What a selfish thing to say. I'm sorry."

"No need to be. I thought the same thing. It's not as if she's a good friend, or even someone we willingly invited."

"What do we do now?"

"You go back to the dining room and act like nothing's wrong while I call the police and the coroner."

"The police? Why the police?"

"I think you have to call them for an unexplained death. Besides, if we don't, what do we *do* with her? Somebody has to take her away to be buried."

Patricia Anne is a sedate suburban housewife living in Birmingham, Alabama, but thanks to her outrageous sister, Mary Alice, she's always in the thick of some controversy, often with murderous overtones. In Murder Shoots the Bull, *Anne George's seventh novel in the Southern Sisters series, the sisters are involved in an investment club with next door neighbor Mitzi. But no sooner have they started the club than strange things start happening to the members . . .*

MURDER SHOOTS THE BULL

by Anne George

I fixed coffee, microwaved some oatmeal, and handed Fred a can of Healthy Request chicken noodle soup for his lunch as he went out the door. Wifely duties done, I settled down with my second cup of coffee and the *Birmingham News*.

I usually glance over the front page, read "People are Talking" on the second, and then turn to the Metro section. Which is what I did this morning. I was reading about a local judge who claimed he couldn't help it if he kept dozing off in court because of narcolepsy when Mitzi, my next door neighbor, knocked on the back door.

"Have you seen it?" She pointed to the paper in my hand when I opened the door.

"Seen what?" I was so startled at her appearance, it took me a moment to answer. Mitzi looked rough. She had on a pink chenille bathrobe which had seen better days and she was barefooted. No comb had touched her hair. It was totally un-Mitzi-like. I might run across the yards looking like this, but not Mitzi. She's the neatest person in the world.

"About the death."

"What death?" I don't know why I asked. I knew, of course. I moved aside and she came into the kitchen.

"Sophie Sawyer's poisoning."

Mitzi walked to the kitchen table and sat down as if her legs wouldn't hold her up anymore.

"Sophie Sawyer was poisoned?"

"Arthur said you were there yesterday."

"I was." I sat down across from Mitzi, my heart thumping faster. "She was poisoned?"

"Second page. Crime reports." Mitzi propped her elbows on the table, leaned forward and put a hand over each ear as if she didn't want to hear my reaction.

I turned to the second page. The first crime report, one short paragraph, had the words—SUS-PECTED POISONING DEATH—as its heading. Sophie Vaughn Sawyer, 64, had been pronounced dead the day before after being rushed to University Hospital from a nearby restaurant. Preliminary autopsy reports indicated that she was the victim of poisoning. Police were investigating.

Goosebumps skittered up my arms and across my shoulders. Sophie Sawyer murdered? Someone had killed the lovely woman I had seen at lunch the day before? I read the paragraph again. Since it was so brief, the news of the death must have barely made the paper's deadline.

"God, Mitzi, I can't believe this. It's awful. Who was she? One of Arthur's clients?"

Mitzi's head bent to the table. Her hands slid around and clasped behind her neck.

"His first wife."

"His what?" Surely I hadn't heard right. Her voice was muffled against the table.

But she looked up and repeated, "His first wife."